The Incident at **Saheb Bagan**

The Incident at
Saheb Bagan

Paushali Ganguli

NIYOGI
BOOKS

Published by

NIYOGI BOOKS

D-78, Okhla Industrial Area, Phase-I
New Delhi-110 020, INDIA
Tel: 91-11-26816301, 49327000
Fax: 91-11-26810483, 26813830
Email: niyogibooks@gmail.com
Website: www.niyogibooks.com

Text©: Paushali Ganguli
Cover illustration: Arindam Chakraborty
Editor: Jyoti Kumari
Design: Arrt Creations

ISBN: 978-93-81523-67-4
Year of Publication: 2013

Printed at: Niyogi Offset Pvt. Ltd., New Delhi, India

There is a real Anand and a real Kammu...and once a real Saheb Bagan...and before the two grow up and forget what they were once like, and they build a housing complex where Saheb Bagan once stood, I had to write about them somewhere so that they remember...

Extraordinary stuff I'm about to write

I don't know if anybody has ever even *remotely* written the kind of stuff that I am about to write now. But one thing I do know, and that is: I absolutely *must* tell you about this because it is the most thrilling and at the same time the scariest thing that has ever happened to me in the whole eleven years of my life.

It's funny, isn't it; how sometimes the most momentous adventure that you can ever imagine begins with a small, ordinary incident? I wish it were possible to point to the event when it happens and say, yes, *now* is the beginning of my fantastic adventure. Let me get prepared for the ride.

Since I couldn't do it that way, I'll tell you, so *you* may be prepared.

Let me give you the background.

Background

It all began the day Jitenkaku came to meet Dad. It was, as usual, a Friday night, 'Open House' day at our place.

My parents' friends seem to think that our house is a station or something. Come Fridays, they all come. Drop in. Weekend...aaaah...and they stretch out on the couch and grab the remote. Some of them start fiddling with my toys. Benumama does that. He always fiddles with my toys if I happen to leave any of them lying around. Especially my Dranzer. It's weird to see an adult playing with beyblades. It completely freaked me out the first time I saw him take my launcher and go wild, whizzing my Dragoon around on the dining table. 'Absolutely cool top. Cool top!' he went on, shaking his head in amazement. *Top*, I tell you! What cheek. It is shameful to watch an adult acting so goofy. Otherwise, as adults go, he's quite ok.

Also, Benumama makes weird friends whom he brings along with him most Fridays. Once he brought home a friend who sold boiled sweets on local trains. His 'run' was from Sealdah to Barrackpore. He stood up in our sitting room and showed us how his spiel went. It went something like this: 'Ladiesandgentlemenbrothersandsistersneicesand nephewsgrandMomsandgrandpopsdoyouknowthe goodnessinthesesweetsthatIamheretosellyoutoday?' Yes, exactly like that. One breathless monologue on the goodness of sweets.

Another time he brought home a friend who is a 'reformed' pickpocket. I asked Mom what a 'reformed pickpocket' was. Mom said he doesn't do it anymore. And please don't ask what he taught me. I liked that friend a lot.

Jitenkaku was the friend that Benumama brought along to our house that night.

'Look who I met in Beadon Street driving a swanky car!' Benumama cried bursting into the sitting room. 'Old Jitu. Remember Jiten? Backbencher in our school? He was always playing dirty tricks on Keshubabu, the Maths teacher? Remember the poem he wrote on the blackboard which got him suspended?'

And Dad stood up in surprise, saying, 'Oh my god! *That* Jiten. How many years has it been? What have you been up to? We must catch up.'

Benumama was still hopping up and down with excitement. 'He almost knocked me down with his car! And when I recognised him, I had to almost *force* him to come!' I noticed that 'Old Jiten' really didn't seem too ecstatic to have been brought to our house, as he smiled around wanly at the assembled guests. But after a couple of hours, he probably got into the swing of things, so to speak and, judging from the sound of laughter and merriment coming from our sitting room, was maybe even beginning to enjoy himself.

And that was the night as I lay in bed trying to cover my ears with a pillow, *striving* to go to sleep (while the gusts of laughter coming from the sitting room made it impossible) fate was at work, bringing me closer and closer to my first serious adventure.

Now, I think I must tell you a bit about my family and myself before I can go any further. Then you will know how difficult it is to be me. And then you will also know how it is only boys like me who can get involved in terrible adventures. But that is my family's fault for bringing me up all wrong.

My Family and I

I am an eleven year old boy. My name is Anand. I am three-fourths Bengali and one-fourth Konkani. That's because my Mom is One Whole Bengali and my Dad is Half Bengali and Half Konkani. That is a lot of Maths.

I am not normal. I do not belong to a normal family. I am highly neglected by my parents. They are very careless about my upbringing. For instance, I just told you how I can never get to sleep on Friday nights. Anybody else's parents would have bothered. Been concerned. Genuinely worried. But my parents? Uh-huh. 'Leave him alone,' says my Dad, 'he'll sleep in the middle of falling bombs if he's sleepy enough.' HA! And my Mom! She went completely berserk on my tenth birthday. 'Double digits!' she kept saying, dancing a jig around the room as she put out my birthday cake on the table, 'Oh dear, he's ten! Double digits!'

And what did my friends see when they came in?

They saw my Mom hugging and kissing me and laughing and crying at the same time. Look. Here's how it is. I *know* her, okay? So I know she gets weird at times. And I don't mind if she does it in private. Like when Dad and I are around. But in front of my friends? It took me a year to recover. I got so traumatised. Traumatised means shocked terribly so you stop being normal.

My parents don't even do things normal parents do. They don't go to office. They don't work like normal parents do. My Mom sits around whole day reading loads and loads of books and roaming around in a daze as if she's somewhere far away. And my Dad sits at his comp browsing the net and chewing the corner of his moustache.

When I was nine, one day I asked them why they didn't go to office like other people. My father looked shocked. 'Why? Why should I go to office? I'm happy here.' My Mom just laughed. 'Don't you think you're lucky? You get to spend so much time with your parents. Who's that friend of yours, that boy you were telling me about—both his parents work and he has to stay at a crèche. It's so sad.'

'*That* boy is Anirudh. He is my best friend. And *his* parents know that I am his best friend and they also happen to know my name.'

'How nice,' said my mother vaguely, drifting away.

'But what do you do?' I asked my father, feeling a little desperate.

'Remember last year and the year before that we had to go away for a couple of months and you had to stay with Dadu and Dida?' asked Dad.

'Yep! Last year Dadu tried to make me do multiplication with three digits and Dida made me learn shlokas. And there was never any chicken and no fish on Sundays and they didn't let me wear...'

'Yes, yes, I know. You've told me. Often. Well, Mom and I make films.'

'Films!' This was worse than anything, *ever*. How could I ever tell my friends? Anirudh's father was a computer engineer and his mother was a dentist. Shyam's dad was a CA. Chirag's dad was a—well he went to office. Ashwat's dad *owned* an office.

'Not *those* kind of films. We make documentary films.'

I was still suspicious. 'You mean those dull and boring things that they show on National Geographic and the History Channel where they go on and on telling you about dead men and old stuff or animals killing each other?'

Dad winced. 'Well, sort of. But we like to think of them as films which give people important information about things that they normally...'

By this time I was halfway out of the room. But I just had to make sure. So I turned back. 'Dad,' I hesitated, 'cross your heart and hope to die you don't really make those singing dancing kissing films? Otherwise I'll *die* in front of my friends. Or I'll tell them you're a spy or something.'

He crossed himself solemnly. 'Cross my heart and hope to die...I make stuff like those shown on National Geographic and the History Channel and after your eleventh birthday you're coming with Mom and me or I know you're going to grow up a moron.'

Looking back on it, I realise that maybe *that* was when all my troubles started. The idea of taking me along was like a seed that sort of got planted in Dad's head. But at that time, I didn't take the last part of what he said seriously. I know grownups don't like traveling with kids. I didn't want to go *traveling* with Mom and Dad. *Living* with them was messy enough. I knew traveling with them would be a nightmare. They are so scatty they would probably lose me somewhere and not even notice until they came back home.

I'd much rather stay with Dadu and Dida. As long as I did my sums and recited the mantras in the morning, I could very much do as I pleased for the rest of the day after school when they were taking care of me. Dida makes good wholesome food. Lots of greens. Karelas and saags. I hate them but I know they are good for me. They help me grow up healthy. Mom doesn't care. She does not touch Dida's greens. 'Ugh,' she said one day making a face, 'I had enough of that when I was a kid. The only reason I wanted to grow up was that I didn't have to touch that yucky stuff again. Poor Andu. I'll make up for it when we come back.' She wouldn't believe me when I told her I didn't mind. She makes food for me without thinking much about the horrible things it does to my body. They create toxins. No greens. No veggies to speak of. Fried chicken dripping in oil. Fish kaliya. Mutton masala. Rogan josh. Biryani. Oh god! Dadu tells me about all the toxins they produce. He has great faith in ayurvedic medicines.

The first week that they come to stay he doses me three times a day with a bitter mixture of several herbs to flush out all the toxins in my body. Then I'm all set for the year.

I do so look forward to their visits.

Back to That Day

Dad introduced me to Jitenkaku later that night when Jitenkaku was feeling more at ease around everybody, and when I had gone in to say goodnight to Dad and Mom. He introduces me to all his friends. I call some of them mama, some kaku, and some jetha. It depends on their age and my mood.

Dad said, 'Jiten, this is my son, Anand. Anand, Jitenkaku. He's an old friend of ours from school.'

Jitenkaku said hello and ruffled my hair and called me cute.

So I'm sure you can tell how much I liked him.

Jitenkaku had a round face. Otherwise there was nothing remotely remarkable about him. He was average: average height, average weight, average skin colour, average voice...the only other remarkable thing about him, apart from his round face, was the ring he wore on the little finger of his right hand. I noticed it when he lifted his hand to ruffle my hair.

It was a gold ring, beaten flat and twisted around like a snake with an open mouth trying to swallow its own tail. I noticed tiny golden fangs in the snake's open mouth. It had one glowing red eye. It was a huge red stone, and I was sure it was a ruby.

I knew rubies. Once, when I was a kid, Dida had shown me an ancient ruby necklace she had been given by *her* mom, and she told me that she was keeping it for my wife. So I knew rubies. And this was a very expensive ruby. But I didn't like the ring. It was creepy and it made me shiver.

Dad told Jitenkaku that I was 'a little bureaucrat' at heart and everybody laughed. I hate jokes that I can't understand. Later on I looked up 'bureaucrat' in the *Oxford Dictionary* and it said, 'government official perceived as being overly concerned with procedural correctness'. I didn't quite get the last part, but I more or less understood the meaning. What was there to laugh at?

I felt a little mad at everybody for having laughed at me. So just to be rude, I asked Jitnkaku, 'What do you do?'

At that Jitenkaku laughed as if I had said something very funny. 'I am a District Magistrate. Do you know what a District Magistrate is?'

I shook my head. Jitenkaku opened his mouth to explain, when Mom interrupted, 'I think this ghost business must be looked into.' Mom doesn't care about who is going to explain what to whom. She sometimes sits quietly in the middle of a conversation with her eyes glazed over, thinking of something someone had said maybe half an hour ago, and then suddenly interrupts as if carrying on the same conversation, not even noticing that people are now talking about something entirely different. Only Dad and I could understand. Dad was okay with this, but it drove me crazy.

Jitnkaku looked startled. I said, 'What ghosts?'

Mom said, 'Jiten's ghosts.'

Dad looked at Mom, 'I think it's late enough already. Anand should be asleep.'

Mom was still in her daydream. 'I think we should go there. Shoot some ghosts.'

Jitenkaku looked acutely unhappy.

Dad looked at me. ANAND. I knew that tone of voice. I turned to walk towards the door. I *tried* to walk slowly but I could only hear Jitenkaku worriedly saying, 'I assure you, it is *most* dangerous. I strongly advise against...' when I couldn't hear any more.

But one thing I was sure of, as I held my pillow hard against my ears to shut out the noise of loud, *raucous* (which means harsh laughter): No one 'strongly advised' my Mom about anything. Especially about dangerous things. And ghosts would, in my book, be one of the **Most Dangerous Things**. She would shoot ghosts if she wanted to, and even if they were dead already she was the sort who would see to it that they got killed again.

It would have taken me much longer to fall asleep that day if I had known that she would drag *me* into it.

How They Dragged Me Into It

By the time Dadu and Dida arrived a week later, I had forgotten about Jitenkaku and shooting ghosts already. I had important things to think about. I had lost my Dranzer. I had fought with Anirudh and we had become enemies for life and I had lost Mom's best pink lipstick which I had borrowed to make a logo for my model tank. So life for me was full of pain and misery.

Mom brought out three suitcases from the musty old closet at the bottom of the stairs instead of the usual two.

No sooner had I hugged Dadu and Dida, when Mom flung one suitcase at my feet and said, 'Pack'.

'Why?' I stared at Dadudida. 'Aren't they here to look after me while you're gone?'

'Nope. Not this time.'

'Then?'

'Listen, Andu, if you want to travel with us, you must learn not to argue and not to ask questions. Just obey the Director's orders.'

'I don't *want* to travel...and who's the Director and it's not even vacations!' Oh my God! Now they wanted me to cut school! What about my interschool debate competition and my mono acting? I looked at Dadudida for help.

'For goodness' sake, anybody would think the boy likes going to school!' Mom appealed to Dad, who was sitting at the coffee table cleaning his cameras.

'Maybe, maybe...' He muttered, polishing his lenses vigourously.

'For god's sake, you're not helping,' snapped Mom turning to go, and then, pointing at the suitcase at my feet, 'Pack!'

'What should I pack? Dad, DAD!'

'Underwear, Andu...never forget the underwear.' He peered at me through a lens.

'And what about my education?'

Dad put down the camera on the table and sighed. 'This fungus...' he muttered, frowning and then looked up at me and blinked, 'what?'

'Nothing. And who's the Director?' I was completely dying with frustration by that time as I didn't think I was about to receive one coherent bit of information from my completely spaced out parent, so I was very surprised when Dad gave me a big grin and twinkled at me. 'Director? Why me, of course!'

Kammu

Kamruddin Sheikh is our driver. I call him Kammu. About nineteen, boots, jeans, metal studded leather belt, hair cut like the latest hit film star, always insisting on speaking in English, and calling Dad 'Sir!' crisply like an army guy—that's our Kammu. He wasn't like this always, of course. He used to repair stolen cars for resale before becoming our driver. His life changed when he had to spend one night in a lock up. He told me that he didn't like it so he became a regular driver. I have sworn a holy oath on the Koran never to tell this to my parents. Otherwise I may die a horrible death. Kammu trusted me with this secret the second day he came to work for us. I had a stomach upset for two days because I just *felt* like telling Mom that night when she came to tuck me in. Imagine how horribly I would have died if I had *told* her.

Kammu told me that I should be prepared. 'Always. You never know.' He said. So I packed my beyblades, my binocs, my laptop, my Swiss knife, my duel master cards, one large tin of aloe vera extract made by Dadu which I faithfully promised to have daily, a packet of Parle-G biscuits in case Mom forgot to feed me (which she often does by the way), my digital camera and my clothes. Mom complained that my bag was heavy. 'What have you got in here', she said, dragging it upto the front door, 'Bricks?'

'Mom,' I said urgently, 'MOM! Mom'

'What?' she snapped, pointing at the bags and muttering things like, 'camera, reflector, four sheets of thermocol, sun gun...'

'Where are we going, and why do we need a gun?' I felt nervous. I had just seen *The Crusades* on TV and I was hoping we wouldn't be going to shoot a war or something.

'Gun? Oh no, it's not *that* kind of gun. It's a light. For shooting.'

'You don't use a gun for shooting but you use a light?' I was completely confused.

'CASSETTES!' my Mom hollered, 'GAUTAM, you've again forgotten the cassettes!'

'What do we need cassettes for?' I asked. 'We have enough music in the car.'

Mom turned to glare at me. She gritted her teeth. 'It's not *that* kind of cassette. It's for...'

I raised my hand to stop her. 'I know. For shooting.'

And I didn't say another word. I just went and sat in the car beside Kammu. They *like* me to be confused. I promised myself that I wouldn't ask another question. If our car had an accident while we were on the way to wherever we were going and I was severely injured and bleeding to death, still I wouldn't ask where we were going. And after I died, Mom would suddenly realise that she hadn't told me and would regret it forever. That will serve them right.

I asked Kammu, 'Where are we going?'

'To a village,' replied Kammu, furiously chewing gum. 'To shoot ghosts.'

'What!' I was shocked. I remembered Jitenkaku and *that* Friday night. Actually I couldn't remember what Jitenkaku looked like at all. I closed my eyes and tried and tried to recollect his face. It wouldn't come. I just knew it was round and brown. But I could clearly remember the snake ring and its glowing eye.

I opened my eyes. Kammu was holding out a stick of gum at me. I popped the gum into my mouth. After all, what the heck. People can't die of cavities.

'A haunted house. Remote village. Ghosts cry at night. Your daddymummy found out. Police found nothing. So we go to shoot. First time in India we shoot live ghosts.' Kammu had probably put four or five sticks of gum into his mouth at one go. He had told me he was trying to give up pan by replacing it with chewing gum.

'Live ghosts? You mean dead ghosts?' I couldn't believe this. My parents were insane! To go on a dangerous mission like this was bad enough, but to take a child with them? I shook my head disbelievingly.

'You don't believe me? Here, take back your money.'

Kammu was miffed. Every time he got miffed he threatened to return my money. I lend him a couple of bucks every week from my pocket money. He never tries to return it unless he is angry with me. He had told me that he never took money from people he did not hold in high esteem. I had to persuade him for *weeks* before he respected me enough to borrow from me.

I didn't want to lose that respect.

Kammu had also told me that he did not respect moneylenders who take interest. 'Taking interest is like eating flesh of respected father,' he had said gravely looking at my money thoughtfully when I had offered it to him. 'They all go to *jahannum*'. I was indignant. Did I look like someone who would eat his father's flesh? I had asked him. He did not respond for a long time. He looked at me and chewed. I waited with a beating heart. After a long while he nodded and held out his hand for the money. I heaved a sigh of relief.

And that's how his respect for me had begun.

But right now he needed to be coaxed into a good mood. And so I said, 'No, no,' I said, 'I believe you. Cross my heart. I just want to know where exactly is this village?'

'Don't know,' said Kammu. 'Your father said "*tankee* full, Kammu" so Kammu did *tankee* full.'

I heaved a sigh of relief. Kammu had forgotten about the money, thank god. I sometimes wished it wasn't this difficult to make people respect you.

Dad and Mom were coming out from the front door shouting last minute instructions to Dadudida inside. Sumit, my next door neighbour and worst enemy, was swinging on his gate watching us. I put out my tongue at him looked away disdainfully to show him that I didn't care that my Mom was carrying thermocol and two half-zipped bags with wires trailing out of them behind her to the car. And that my Dad was carrying two equally large bags and tripping over the trailing wires as he followed her. What else can one do to defend the *izzat* of parents like mine? They just don't get the concept of family honour.

I remember once when Anirudh had brought home a new video game for me to try out. We were playing peacefully, when Dad and Mom drifted into the room. They stopped and looked. I ignored them, hoping that like all parents they would also go away after some time. But no. They stayed. And after sometime they started telling us what to do. 'Andu, the left. The LEFT! Hit him from the left...oh no!' types...and before I knew what was happening, we were the ones standing, while the two of them were sitting with the controls in their hands. And as we watched them aghast, they shouted and cheered, egging each other on. *And* they did high fives. Family honour? Ha!!!

I sighed. My life was very complicated. It seemed that we were off.

Before Kammu started the engine, I got off to make sure that they had loaded my bag. Mom said she's never seen such a fuss. When I was satisfied, I climbed back into the car again and Kammu smiled at me before he put the key in the ignition. He had coated his front teeth with a membrane of the pink gum and it looked as if his gums had grown down over his front teeth. I got such a shock, I can't tell you.

He kept smiling his gummy smile at me sweetly while he started the car. I glared at him. Mom grumbled at me. I glared at her. The car moved away from our house. I looked back and scowled at Sumit who waggled his ears at me. Dadudida were standing at the front door, waving at us. I think Dadudida thought I was scowling at them. Now I knew I'd feel guilty all my life that I made my old grandparents feel bad before going away—perhaps never to return. Then whenever they remembered their last glimpse of me, they would think of my scowly face. I felt like weeping. But I swallowed hard and gritted my teeth and kept quiet. I promised myself that ghosts or no ghosts, I could not afford to die on this trip and make Dadudida feel bad for the rest of their old lives.

This cheered me up somewhat and I began to even feel a little excited at whatever lay ahead of us. We were off on an adventure and I was determined to come out of it alive.

Remote Village

We reached the 'remote village' without bumping into any trucks, cars or cows, to my utter relief, though Kammu tried his hardest. It's a wonder my parents don't fire him. In fact, at the end of the journey, when we were driving up to the front gate of the Dak Bungalow, Mom looked at her watch.

'9 o'clock. We've made it in excellent time!' she gushed, 'well done, Kammu! I would have hated to arrive in the middle of the night.'

I thought this was a bit too much. 60 kms speed limit. That was what the signs on the rutted track they call a highway stated. Kammu's hairraising speeds, besides being bad for my heart, were completely illegal. And she was aiding and abetting an illegal act by encouraging him, besides being downright inconsiderate towards my wellbeing.

The Dak Bungalow was a spooky place, covered all over, as far as one could see in the car headlights through the grilled iron gate, with creepers and ferns of all kinds. It had a tiled roof, covered with bougainvillea, and a roofed in porch with white railings running all around it. Though I couldn't see the back of the house from where we were sitting, I guessed the porch would continue round to the back too.

Something like this.

If you draw a rectangle within a rectangle, then the first rectangle would be the porch, like a moat, all around the house, and the second rectangle would be the house itself. Now cover the whole thing with lots of dark green, with occasional mad dashes of red and white, and you would have the ferns and the bougainvillea. Kammu switched off the car engine and the headlights, and suddenly it became very very quiet all around. Then slowly I realised that there was an intense sound all around and about and inside my head. A kind of continuous ringing.

'Cicadas', said Dad, his voice sounding very loud

because of the stillness all around.

Everyone breathed. Strange, how everyone has a different way of breathing, Dad's was long and slow and soothing, Mom's slightly quicker and a little excited...

'Sir!' I jumped out of my skin. Kammu's voice was like a pistol shot in my ear. I saw that he was pointing at a glimmer of bobbing light coming through the dense shrubbery around the house towards the gate. The light shifted and bobbed, coming closer and closer to us and then suddenly an oldish man stepped out of the tangled mess of a garden onto the path in front of the house which led up to the gate. He was holding a hurricane lantern high above his head for maximum light. Even from inside the car, I could see that the chimney was filthy. The old man hobbled upto the gate and with a lot of grunting and groaning, managed to push it open for us. I wondered whether the old man had gout. I knew about gout. Otherwise why was he grunting and groaning so much. He wasn't *that* old. The gate also protested, rattling and squeaking as if it was angry at being woken up. As our car went past him to the house, the headlights swept over the old man's face. He looked harmless enough, like any old chowkidar, down to his dhoti, shawl and monkey cap, but something in his expression made me shiver. He was glaring at the car, his eyes glittering with hate in the light of the lantern.

I looked back and saw him spitting towards our car before he turned back to shut the loudly protesting gate.

The chowkidar's name was Jamirbhai. Mom asked him when he came to ask us what we would like for dinner and to distribute hurricane lanterns. Why he had to ask us I don't know since all he had was chicken. And all he said he could cook was chicken curry. We had dinner on the front porch where Jamirbhai laid out a cane table with a stained green plastic tablecloth and three chairs. The plates and bowls containing rice and chicken were cracked but clean. I checked. Mom lit a mosquito coil and placed it on the railing near the table. Jamirbhai hung a hurricane lamp from the eaves of the ceiling. After serving us, he went away, while we tucked into the piping hot curry and rice. It was delicious, and eating in the dim, flickering light of the lamp made me feel like Obelix at his village party. I was almost happy.

Then Mom said she liked Jamirbhai. 'He seems very nice, don't you think?' she asked Dad. Dad nodded, his mouth full.

'I think there's something sinister about him,' I remarked darkly.

Mom's eyes laughed at me. 'Oh Andu, you always find something sinister about everybody.'

'You're not sinister.'

'If you met me here for the first time today, you'd think I was sinister.'

'No,' I protested. 'You look...kind of...tame. Though your hair looks a bit wild.'

She reached out across the table and ruffled my hair. 'Sometimes I think you *like* being ghoulish.'

I hate it when she ruffles my hair. It makes it stick up in all directions. But now I was feeling full and sleepy, so I smiled at her. Sometimes I like Mom. And Dad. After all, it is not their fault they're grown up.

The Next Morning

Next morning, I woke up quite early, feeling a little stiff. I looked up at the high beamed cobwebby ceiling and the squeaky fan and remembered that we were in our 'Bhootvillage'. I still didn't know the real name of the place. I had been too tired last night to even look at the milestones and signposts and towards the end of the journey had just concentrated on keeping my teeth inside my mouth, the jarring had gotten so awful. I got out of bed and noticed that someone had placed my bag on the table beside the bed. The mosquito coil had burnt itself out into a little pile of ash in the corner of the room. The hurricane lamp on the table was still flickering and I blew it out, remembering that Mom had insisted I don't blow it out at night. 'It's a new place and you might need to go to the loo or something,' she had said. I was too tired to argue. I was almost sure that if the place caught fire, Mom and Dad would rescue me since they were just next door. To tell you the truth I was rather glad of the light when they tucked me in and went off to their own room. The last thing I remember before falling off to sleep is the noise of the cicadas and the huge shadow of the jug of water flickering gently on the wall near my foot.

I got out of bed. The stone floor felt cold. Someone had kept my rubber slippers on the floor beside the bed. I wore them and flopped out of the room. Dad was already awake, sitting at the cane table on the front porch, still in his pyjamas, drinking tea. 'It's cold,' I complained, shivering slightly. 'It's September,' Dad shrugged. 'Bracing. You'll feel warm and tingly after you have a bath in the water from the well here.'

'Water from the well?' This was clearly not my day. 'What about the mosquito larvae that live in stagnant water?'

'Yohoo! My god! What a lovely morning!' That was my dear Mom with her perfect sense of timing.

'The birds are screeching their heads off,' I grumped. 'Yesterday, cicadas. Today, screechy birds.

One would think there would be some peace and quiet in the countryside.'

'I take it you've slept well,' Mom laughed at me.

'So-so,' I shrugged.

'Look Andu,' she pointed. 'How the cobweb looks with the dew glittering on its strands. Have you ever seen anything so beautiful? And the trees look washed and clean. Everything is so GREEN!' She flung her arms wide and breathed deeply.

I looked around. The day did look rather greeny bluey misty dampish. And the sunlight was glinting golden yellow. Not bad. Like a freshly painted watercolour whose colours were still runny. The Dak Bungalow didn't look spooky at all in the early morning light. Just a little old and neglected.

I spied Jamirbhai making his way towards the Dak Bungalow through a faint path in the wild overgrowth of the garden. He was carrying an enormous tin bucket. He was also, unlike us, well wrapped up in his shawl and monkey cap. And this morning, he had changed into a pair of dark blue thick looking trousers. He was wise.

'Jamirbhai!' Dad cupped his hand to his mouth and hollered. Jamirbhai paused. 'Keep the bucket near the well. THE WELL!'

Jamirbhai nodded and sheered off the path into the jungle.

'Well!' My Mom's eyes shone. 'Let's take a bath in well water.'

'That was the idea,' said Dad.

'Why can't we take a bath in the bathroom?' That was me.

'It'll be an experience which you'll look back on in the years to come. Trust me,' said Dad. I sighed.

It was true. The first douche of cold water is something I'm not likely to forget even in my next birth. I yowled. Dad laughed and douched me with another bucket of water. I yelped. Then I threw a bucket of water at Dad but Mom got in the way. She yelped. Then we all went crazy. We had a kind of mad well-water fight dousing each other with buckets of the ice cold water. The area around the well was paved with cobblestones which had become mossy with age. We danced around in our rubber slippers slipping and sliding about, grabbing at each other for balance, trying to reach for the rope to pull up the filled bucket from the well. As soon as one of us hoisted the bucket up, the other two would grab at it and try to pour it over each other. We never really filled the big bucket that Jamirbhai left for us. When we had had enough, we went back to the bungalow, shivering in our wet clothes.

After a huge breakfast of double omelettes made of ducks' eggs, *tawa* toasted bread and butter, and hot milky coffee, we went out to explore the village. Kammu came along with us. Last night he had slept in the car after his dinner, and today he had already bathed and done a round around the village. 'Very beautiful,' he said, chewing the stem of a white flower, as he walked along beside us, 'like a *photu*. Not look like Bhootvillage.'

I got a mild shock. I had forgotten about the *bhoots*. They were what we were here for. 'Kammu,' I asked, 'what is the name of this village?'

'Shantighat.' Kammu laughed. 'Strange name for a village full of *ashant bhoots*, right?'

Shantighat

'I want to tell you something about this village, so listen carefully,' said Dad to me as we started off for the village. Dad was carrying his 'shooting' camera. I had hidden mine in my jacket pocket.

Mom had proposed that we walk. I had proposed that we drive. Mom won because she's older and a bit of a bully. I was still feeling miffed that I had lost to her in the arm wrestling competition to decide which mode of transport we would use.

So I did what I wouldn't have ordinarily done. I recited, 'Name of village: Shantighat. 30 kms away from the Indo-Bangladesh border. Nearest big town: Bongaon. During Partition many refugees from across the border took, err, refuge in this area. In fact they passed through here on their way to Kolkata. Now it is just another quiet, ordinary Indian village except for a bit of smuggling which happens now and then between India and Bangladesh.'

Dad stared at me, his mouth open. I looked away, trying to look modest. I caught Kammu's eye and winked at him. He winked back. After I lost to Mom, he had whispered all this information into my ear and had told me, 'Magicians always have extra card. Hidden from all. Try out when you get chance. Next time I teach you how to win arm wrestling. No time now.' I had lent him two bucks in exchange. I felt that it was money well spent.

Mom looked at me admiringly, 'Smart kid. I told you he'd find out before we told him.'

'Apart from the quiet, ordinary Indian village, you've got the rest of it right,' said Dad.

'Tell me the rest, Dad,' I wanted to know.

'There is a bungalow on the border of Bamunpara and Musalman *patti* in this village called Saheb Bagan. It is said to be haunted. The story goes that after independence, the Saheb refused to leave for England because he felt that India had become his country. But one day, his wife took their two children and tried to go to England. On their way, they were captured by bandits and after that they disappeared. The Saheb lived on here, and is said to have died of a broken heart. They say that his ghost is still searching for his missing wife and children. And they also say that his wife and children, who died while they were prisoners of the bandits, also keep crying and looking for the Saheb so that he can rescue them.'

'That's sad,' I thought for a while. 'Are you here to shoot these ghosts?'

Dad frowned. 'Did you tell anybody we're here to shoot ghosts?'

'No. Who would I tell? Jamirbhai? He's the only person I've met since we arrived,' I said.

'Don't tell him. Don't tell anyone. We're here as tourists. Tracing our roots and all that,' said Dad waving his hands airily. 'You know how people go back to the villages where their great great great grandfather was the local Raja or a big zamindar or something and write books about it? Like that.'

'Or maybe the village idiot?' Mom suggested helpfully. Dad glared at her. She slipped behind me giggling as Dad swiped at her. He almost took my eye off. Adults!

Dad continued, 'We don't want to be known as documentary filmmakers. Then people will either get self conscious or clam up on us.'

'But you're carrying the camera.'

'This looks like an ordinary video camera, not that the people here will know the difference. And I'm a stupid tourist. I shoot anything that takes my fancy. You're the stupid son of a stupid tourist, okay?' said Dad.

'Okay,' I said, trying my best to look stupid. It wasn't easy.

'So can I shoot with my camera?' I asked after a couple of minutes of trying to look stupid, taking my digital camera out of my jacket pocket. The muscles of my face had started to ache by then.

'Of course. Concentrate on interesting faces. I'll use your stills if they're good. But keep your mouth shut. And stop making faces. You look like a stupid fool.'

I opened my mouth to protest. I was following orders. *His* orders. I now knew why loyal army jawans gave such bitter interviews on TV. They followed orders and look what it got them. I felt bitter. Kammu snickered. I glared at him.

By this time we had entered the village. There was a dusty rutted road lined on both sides with quaint little shops. They were either tiled or thatched and sold a variety of things from colourful dresses, handkerchiefs and bedsheets to sweetmeats and foodstuffs. Loud film music was blaring from the shops. People were buying vegetables heaped on the roadside on plastic sheets. There was also a cycle repair shop and next to it a shop which sold tea and rice plate with fish. The insides of all these shops looked cool and dark and mysterious. By this time, the sun was quite warm and under the golden light and the deep blue autumn sky and the dark green trees with their dreamy shadows, it looked like a village out of a fairy tale.

'This is the marketplace,' said Dad. 'There are generally two kinds of markets in villages.'

'I know.' I said, 'the *haat* and the *bajaar*.'

'Good. The *haat* is generally weekly or twice a week and is almost like a fair. It is held mostly on open ground with makeshift stalls. The *bajaar* is permanent. Like this one.'

'What are you going to shoot here, Dad,' I whispered.

'Watch.' Dad turned to look at Mom who lifted her eyebrows at him. He jerked his head slightly at the stalls where people had just begun to notice us and to stop and stare. Mom nodded slightly and began walking casually towards the shops. Dad lifted his camera as if to shoot. By craning my neck over his shoulder, I could see that Dad had tilted his viewfinder slightly away from her so he was actually shooting the shops and the people while it looked like he was photographing Mom.

'I'm shooting the general ambience of the market-place. It is important, Andu, to show your audience where you are. So they can be there with you.'

'But people are looking at the camera.' I was also clicking away.

'That's always the trouble,' sighed Dad. 'I'm trying to leave them out. Thankfully only a few people have noticed us till now.'

'Dad, look!' Suddenly I saw a peculiar figure emerging around the corner of one of the shops. He was dressed in a blood red dhoti and shawl and had a number of *rudraksha* necklaces around his neck. His hair was thick and shaggy, unwashed and uncombed. It was completely matted with grime. His beard reached upto his waist and it was equally matted and dirty. His eyes were red and he had a red *tilak* on his forehead. He was holding a *trishul* in one hand and a *lota* in the other.

'What a character!' Dad enthused, turning his camera on the guy. 'Got him! Did you get him, Andu?'

'I got four clear shots!' I was hopping with excitement.

'Good show!' and he slapped me on the back.

'He's a tantrik,' muttered Kammu. 'Sir, he live in jungle behind Saheb Bagan. He make *bhoot* go away when people get fright. He tame *bhoot*.'

Dad stared at Kammu. 'He's the one they call Pretsiddha.' He looked at me. 'It means that they can make ghosts do whatever they want. His name is Haru Tantrik. He used to be a *gunda* when he was young.'

'How do you know all this?' I was surprised.

'Jitenkaku told me. You remember Jiten?'

'Yes. Benumama's friend.'

'He's the District Magistrate of this area. This village is under his charge. I'm sure he knows everything about all the *gundas* and other weirdos who live here. He would naturally know all the legends and superstitions too.'

'Dad, what's a District Magistrate?'

'Sort of like the head of government in this area.'

'Dad, why didn't he come with us?'

'He had urgent work in Kolkata. Government stuff,' he waved his hand vaguely. 'He arranged for us to stay in the Dak Bungalow when he realised that your mother was determined to come here.'

'Didn't he want us to come?'

'No.'

'Why?'

'Stop asking so many questions, Andu,' Dad sounded exasperated. 'He probably didn't want strangers to poke their nose in his jurisdiction. He probably thought it was dangerous.' Dad shrugged.

I didn't feel at all reasurred.

Haru Tantrik and the Riceplate Man

By this time Haru Tantrik had walked up to the centre of the marketplace almost upto the riceplate restaurant.

'*Bom Bhole. Kali Kaaali Tara maaaa...*' He boomed. I trained my camera on him. The riceplate owner came to the entrance of his shop, wiping his hands on a towel. He walked up to Haru and doing a *namaskar*, dropped a coin into Haru's *lota*. I zoomed in on them. Through the camera viewfinder, I thought I distinctly saw Haru muttering something at the Riceplate Man. The Riceplate Man glanced nervously over his shoulder at us, just as I pressed the shutter.

Haru Tantrik acknowledged the contribution with a regal nod of his fantastic head and turned to go. We watched him make his dignified way back out of the marketplace bowing now and then whenever people came forward to drop a coin or two into his *lota*. It occurred to me that any American popstar wanting to grow major dreadlocks could take a tip or two from this guy. He could make a lot of money advising them on how to grow them just right. No combing for three weeks, he would say. And then a light dusting of dandruff and grime. And twist it around with your fingers just so, before you go to bed every night. Dreadlock Consultant, he could have printed on his card. He could become a millionaire in no time.

After Haru Tantrik's *filmi* exit, we took a few more desultory shots of the people and the marketplace, and then we went into the Riceplate Man's shop for tea. It was a small shop with mud walls and beaten mud floor, with several wooden benches and tables neatly arranged.

The Riceplate Man came into the shop from another room at the back, wiping his hands.

'Babu,' he joined his hands together and smiled with pan-stained teeth. 'You have come to this poor man's shop. What can I give you?'

Dad ordered tea for all of us. The Riceplate Man bent almost double over his folded hands and nodded his round head.

I did not like him. He had wispy greyish hair, a perfectly round head, a greyish dirty stubble, and was wearing stained white pyjamas and kurta. And he seemed to be a bit too eager and happy to please us city slickers. His smile was too wide and did not reach his eyes which were calculating and cold.

I suddenly felt pee-ish. Dad told me to go out the back way. 'You'll probably find a bush or something far enough,' he said.

I got up to go. The inside of the shop was dark and you had to turn right and walk along a small passage before you could see the outside. On the left was the open door of the kitchen, full of a lot of stained iron pots and pans. I glanced in as I passed. The Riceplate Man was leaning over the kettle on the *chullah,* his back towards me. In the far corner I could see the huddled figure of a man lying asleep. It was dim and I couldn't see his face clearly, but as I hesitated I heard him give a loud snore. The Riceplate Man quickly glanced at him and then towards the door where I was standing. For a moment his eyes glittered and his lips curled back over his mouth in an angry snarl. 'What do you want here?' he almost spat at me. I was taken aback. 'I'm going to do bathroom,' I pointed towards the end of the passage. At once the man's face changed into a servile smile. 'Of course, of course, Babu...' I saw him glance again at the sleeping man out of the corner of his eyes. 'Who is he?' I burst out before I could stop myself. The Riceplate Man hesitated and I saw him glancing this way and that as if looking for a way to escape. Finally, he wetted his lips and said, 'He is Bablu's father. You know, the boy next door in the cycle repair shop.'

'Why is he sleeping so late?' I asked, 'Is he ill?'

The Riceplate Man nodded vigorously, the kettle in his hand bobbing up and down. He looked suddenly relieved, 'Yes, Choto Babu. He is ill.' I went off to pee feeling sure the man was lying.

When I came back, tea had been served. Kammu sat at a table a little away from us and flipped a coin while he drank his tea. Dad and Mom spoke of nothing in particular. I was puzzled and kept silent. The tea was awful.

After tea, as we left the shop, I deliberately hung back a little, pretending to tie my shoelaces while letting Mom and Dad go on ahead. When they were out of hearing distance, I walked on up to the cycle repair shop next to the tea stall and looked at the little boy working on the doorstep. He looked at me and glanced away quickly, bending down as if to concentrate more on what he was doing. I looked back to see whether the Riceplate Man was watching. He wasn't. He had probably gone inside.

'Hey, Bablu,' I called, 'your name is Bablu, I know.'

The boy stopped his work but didn't look up.

'Why is your father sleeping in the kitchen of the teashop? Is he ill?' I asked.

Bablu quickly looked up at me, his eyes wide, 'he's come back then?' he asked.

'Come back? From where?' I was puzzled.

Bablu quickly glanced behind my shoulder, looking afraid. I looked back and saw the Riceplate Man watching us from the entrance of his shop. He looked furious. I walked away from the shop casually, my hands in my pockets, whistling innocently.

'Hurry up,' Dad said, as I caught up with him. 'We need to visit Saheb Bagan.'

As I walked along beside him, my mind buzzed with questions. Why did the Riceplate Man lie about Bablu's father and tell me that he was ill? Was he really ill? If so, why wasn't he sleeping next door in his own shop? And why did Bablu not know that his father was in the teashop? And what did he mean by 'He's come back?' Come back from where? And why was the Riceplate Man so angry at my talking to Bablu? Who was Haru Tantrik? Why was he so friendly with the Riceplate Man? What was he telling him when I shot the two of them?

Now I was really confused. But the thing that niggled at me most was this: What were my parents up to? Had they really come to shoot ghosts?

Saheb Bagan

We were standing in front of massive iron gates. They were the most massive, the most rusted and the most locked gates I had seen in my whole life. They were as tall as a small coconut tree and attached to two huge marble pillars on either side with hinges as thick as my thighs. The rust made them look red and I counted as many as five locks attached to chains as thick as my wrists wound around the grills. The locks were dirty with dry mud encrusted on them as if they had been untouched for a long time. A high wall ran along either side of the gate, sheer and mossy, impossible to climb. So *this* was Saheb Bagan.

Dad whistled, 'Someone doesn't want us to be here.'

'We should have asked Jiten for the keys,' said Mom.

'How should he have the keys,' said Dad, 'this is private property.'

'Whose property is it?' I asked, 'Let's go ask *him*.'

'Do you know,' said Dad slowly, looking down at me, 'I should have asked Jiten who owns Saheb Bagan. And do you know that I'm so stupid that it never once occurred to me?'

'Well, let's ask him then,' I said. 'Let's call him, or go to his office or something. He's the District Magistrate of this place, isn't he? He must have an office or something nearby. Someone might know the owner, or have the keys,' I said hopefully.

'It may not be ok to go to his office while he's not here,' said Mom. 'He may not like to have his staff know why we're here. And we don't know his mobile number.'

'Or if he *has* a mobile,' said Dad.

'He should have come with us,' said Mom.

'Oh come on, Maya,' said Dad, 'he can't cancel meetings with the Home Minister just because *you* wanted him to come with us.'

'Home Minister,' Mom snorted. 'A likely story. If you ask me, he wanted to avoid coming with us.'

'Now why would he do that? You're beginning to sound like Andu.'

Mom didn't reply. She just snorted and tossed her head.

The four of us (don't forget Kammu) silently stared at the locked gates. There didn't seem to be anything that we could do just now.

'The wall seems to run endlessly along both sides,' said Mom after sometime, 'but they must end somewhere. I heard there are huge jungles at the back of the house for miles. The wall surely can't enclose the jungles. There must be gaps somewhere.'

I had my head pressed against the grills of the gate and was straining to get a glimpse of the *baari* (that's the Bengali in me, *baari* is house!). I could make out the rambling outlines of a huge bungalow through the overgrown trees and shrubbery which blocked out most of the sunlight. The house, what I could see of it through the thick leaves, was a warm brick red in colour. I could just make out, if I twisted my neck far to the right, a window with silver shutters. The house looked like a glowing red jewel set in the middle of a dense, dark jungle. A leaf-strewn path twisted its way towards the house, but disappeared amongst dense shrubs around a corner. I tried to get a shot of the house by reaching inside the grills and focusing my camera on it as best as I could, but my hand slipped and the camera fell inside the gates, on the dried leaves of the path.

I kneeled down and tried to stretch my hand inside as far as I could, but the camera was just out of my reach. 'Kammu,' I shouted, turning to him, and out of the corner of my eyes, I spied something which made my heart go cold. It was a white handkerchief, a big white handkerchief used by men, with the letter 'Z' embroidered on it with dark blue thread. It was fluttering way inside the grounds, twisted around the stem of a small shrub with red flowers. Who had dropped it? And how did he get inside? The ground all around and inside the gates was dry and covered with fallen leaves, and the handkerchief was clean, not mudstained. This made me feel that it must not have been dragged along the ground by the breeze. It *must* have been dropped by someone inside.

Kammu had to stretch his hand *wayyyy* inside before he could even reach the camera strap. He dragged it towards him bit by bit and when it was near enough, caught hold of it.

'Here,' he said, tossing it towards me. I caught it neatly. I'm quite a good *catcher*, you know. I can catch almost anything. Dad says I've got good reflexes. Why, once...never mind...will save that story for some other day. The important point here was that the camera was safe. I was glad that the ground was covered with dry leaves and had cushioned the camera's fall, so there was no chance that the camera was damaged. In fact, as I held it in my hands looking at its glistening chrome and steel body, something niggled at the back of my mind. There was something odd here, I felt, which I ought to remember. Which didn't fit. Which was a clue...to what, I didn't know...but it was definitely something that didn't fit. And I wasn't thinking of the handkerchief.

The Old Man

While coming to Saheb Bagan my mind had been buzzing with questions about Haru Tantrik, Riceplate Man and Bablu, so I had hardly noticed our surroundings. Now, as we walked back towards the Dak Bungalow, I was more aware of the beautiful countryside all around us.

The dusty and rutted red clay road that we were

walking along was lined on both sides with big shady trees. The sky overhead was cloudless, and an incredible blue. The sunlight glinting on the leaves made them look waxed and clean.

We passed a huge banyan tree with its girth so wide that a biggish hut could easily fit into it. Its coarse brown vines hung so low that some of them almost brushed my head. There was deep shade and utter silence under the tree except for the far off ooo-kuk-kuk-kuk-kuk call of some strange bird.

'This tree must be a hundred years old,' whispered Dad in awe.

'Probably more,' hissed back Mom.

I knew why they were whispering. Even I felt it. It was as if the world was drowsing and the great tree stood guard to see that no one disturbed the peace. Kammu looked uneasy. He was shifting from one foot to the other and looking up into the branches of the tree.

I sidled up to him. 'Whatsamatter?' I whispered, 'Afraid of crow shit?'

'N-o,' he said uneasily, not quite meeting my eyes.

'Then?'

'Don't like banyan trees,' he said, now looking at me, trying to give what he probably thought was a casual shrug. 'Shouldn't stand under. Anything might happen.'

I opened my mouth to ask what could possibly happen, when he quickly pressed his hand on my mouth. 'Don't open. Wide mouth. Anything go in, stay there.'

I shook my head free. 'You're afraid I might swallow something falling down from above?'

Kammu shook his head. 'Not something. Someone.'

'What?'

'Spirit. Djinn.' Kammu was still glancing around uneasily. 'Open mouth. Djinn go in stomach, stay there. You become someone else.'

My heart quivered. I didn't believe it, I told myself. But under the dark heavy shade of that huge brooding tree, where you could almost *feel* the silence, a part of me felt that it just *could* happen, you never know. I thought I could hear soft muffled footsteps approaching. I clutched Kammu in alarm.

'Kammu, can you hear that,' I breathed into his ear.

'Yes,' he whispered back. 'Shhh...'

While Kammu and I were talking, we had been slowly circling the tree and had come around almost to the opposite side from where we couldn't see the road. Mom and Dad were also on the jungle side, a few yards away from us, still admiring the tree. The footsteps, muffled by the thick grass, seemed to be coming around towards us. I clutched Kammu's arm hard. And then we saw him.

He was an old man with a shock of white hair on his head, a flowing white beard, holding a cane walking stick. He was wearing a white dhoti and kurta and new floaters. He looked quite dramatic. He came around the tree and peered at us in surprise.

'Hello, hello, hello,' he said in a high-pitched voice, swishing his cane about in front of him. 'So these are the visitors, eh?' and he peered at me. I stared back at him, feeling suddenly foolish at having been so scared a few seconds before. I let go of Kammu's arm. Dad and Mom came up. Somehow, the entrance of this funny, slightly ridiculous old man had broken the deep mysterious spell that had held me in thrall under the tree. Everything seemed ordinary, somehow normal and every day, again.

Dad and Mom greeted the old man politely. 'I was just passing by,' said the old man 'and I saw the three of you walking around the tree. We have very few visitors in our village. Did you come from Saheb Bagan? Did you see anything?' The old man seemed terribly eager to hear Dad's answer.

Dad explained to him that the gates were locked so we hadn't been able to see anything.

I stared hard at the old man. Had I seen him

somewhere before? The market perhaps? But if I had seen him, I would surely have remembered. All that hair would make it hard for me to forget him. Also, he had said he had seen the 'three' of us walking around the tree. We were four, if you included Kammu. *He* obviously wasn't including Kammu. Which meant that he had taken one look at him and decided that since Kammu was our driver, he was of 'servant' category, and not to be included while referring to us. The old man was obviously a snob. I decided I didn't like him. I tugged at Kammu's arm.

'Let's go, Kammu,' I whispered.

The old man was still talking to Mom and Dad. We walked around the banyan tree and out onto the road again. I was beginning to feel hungry.

'I'm hungry,' I told Kammu.

Kammu nodded. He looked at the Mickey Mouse watch on his wrist that I had given him on his birthday and said, 'One o' clock. Lunchtime. Come. Walk fast. Daddymummy will know we go dakbungalow.'

I started running. 'Last one who reaches is a chicken,' I shouted at Kammu over my shoulder.

Kammu said, 'Wait!'

'Chicken, chicken, chicken,' I chanted as I ran harder.

I could hear Kammu's pounding footsteps

behind me. 'Wait, wait, you chicken. You running wrong way.'

'You're just saying that to make me stop so you can catch up,' I panted.

'No, no,' Kammu sounded urgent. 'You run *to* Saheb Bagan. Market that way,' he said, pointing behind us. '*Allah Kasam*!'

I slowed down. 'What did you say?'

'You chicken. Market *ulta* way. You again reach Saheb Bagan. We be late for lunch.'

Kammu was probably right. He never joked about food. I stopped and looked around, frowning. I *was* running the wrong way. The road did look kind of familiar. And then I noticed something strange. There was a dusty jeep parked on the side of the road near us. It was almost hidden by the hedge. I was almost sure there wasn't a jeep parked here when we were walking back from Saheb Bagan.

'Kammu, look,' I said, walking up to the jeep.

I peered inside. There was no driver.

Kammu tugged at my arm. 'Come. Lunchtime.'

I turned to go back the way we had come. I kept quiet until we reached the banyan tree. I could hear the faint murmur of voices coming from the other side of the tree. Which meant that Dad and Mom were still there talking to the funny old man. I opened my mouth after we had left the tree safely behind.

'Kammu,' I asked, as I jogged along beside him, 'Did you notice the jeep when we were walking back from Saheb Bagan?'

'No.' Kammu jogged a little faster.

'Why would a jeep be parked in the middle of nowhere?'

'Not nowhere. Border of Bamunpara and Musalman *patti*.'

'But nobody lives here. This is all empty fields and jungle,' I waved my hands around to demonstrate.

Kammu looked down at me scornfully. 'Nobody live in border. Houses start kilometer this side and kilometer that side of border. Two–three kilometer border area empty. Only Saheb Bagan. Saheb must be fool. Maybe jeep man go to piss piss.'

'Why was Saheb a fool?' I was panting by now. I could see the shops of the marketplace at a distance.

'Delivery men have to travel long. Less money *saaman* will not deliver.' Kammu grinned.

'He probably sent his driver to the village to buy groceries,' I said. 'And I don't think jeep man go piss piss. I think there was no jeep man.'

Kammu looked down at me, sweating and panting and slowed down to a walk. 'Then what? Bhoot?'

'I think the jeep belongs to the old man. He wasn't "passing by" at all,' I said, holding my sides to ease the stitch there. 'He must have followed us all the way from Saheb Bagan, at a distance, parked the jeep on the side of the road, and then walked briskly to catch up with us near the banyan tree. We were lucky I went the wrong way.'

'Why old man like that lie?'

'I don't know Kammu. I wish now that I had stayed to listen to what he had to say.'

'Why not ask daddymummy at dakbungalow?'

I stared at Kammu. 'Good, idea, Kammu,' I said. Something had just flashed across my mind. 'And Kammu,' I asked slowly, 'have you seen an old man wearing floaters?'

Invited to an 'adult' meeting

After a long and leisurely lunch of Jamirbhai's delicious chicken curry and rice, I sat back with a sigh.

'Andubabu full?' asked Mom, smiling at me.

I was full. I rubbed my stomach and burped. Dad laughed. 'There's your answer. Now, in my room in five minutes. We have much to discuss.'

I felt sleepy. 'Me too?' I asked in surprise. Never had I been called in for an 'adult' meeting before.

'Of course. Are you or are you not a part of the team?' asked Dad.

'Kammu also?' I asked.

'Even Kammu,' said Dad, pushing back his chair and getting up. 'So you may go and tell him to come here pronto.'

The 'Meeting'

I downloaded the images from my digicam onto my laptop and the four of us poured over them in my room. The ones of the marketplace were pretty good. There were also some wonky shots of Saheb Bagan through the gates before I had dropped the camera, but since they only showed the locked gates, and not much of the house, they weren't very exciting. There were some close ups of the gate and the huge muddy locks which I promptly sent into the recycle bin. Dad kept on pausing at the shot of the Riceplate Man and Haru Tantrik.

'There's something going on here. Something that smells fishy,' said Dad.

'It's not only ghosts, is it Dad?' I asked him.

'No', sighed Dad. 'It's not only ghosts. That's just a local legend. But I do have a feeling that something is going on, at least between those two,' he said, pointing at a photograph of Haru Tantrik and the Riceplate Man.

'But we don't *know* anything, do we really?'

said Mom.

'No,' said Dad, looking worried. 'I just hope it isn't anything dangerous.' He looked at Mom. 'If so, I wouldn't like the two of you getting mixed up in this.'

'What exactly did Jitenkaku tell you about this place, Dad?' I asked.

'Jiten told me that his office had reports of strange sounds and sights in this area especially around Saheb Bagan. The rumours about the ghosts started about the same time. And also about the same time, Haru Tantrik was released from prison after serving time for armed robbery. This was about three years ago.'

'So you think there is a connection between the three?'

Dad shrugged. 'What would *you* think?'

'I would think,' I said slowly, working something out in my head, 'that there is definitely something going on between those two,' I pointed at the shot of Haru Tantrik and the Riceplate Man. 'And I'll tell you something else.'

And I told them all about Bablu's father and how I had found him lying asleep in the Riceplate Man's kitchen and how he had told me he was ill. And how Bablu had asked me whether he had 'come back'.

There was a long silence after my story. Dad and Mom looked at each other, and then they both looked at me. At last Dad cleared his throat. 'Well.

There certainly is a mystery here.' Mom nodded vigorously. We also discussed the handkerchief with the 'Z' on it, but Dad dismissed it as a 'weak' clue.

'Weak or not,' said Mom, 'we ought to keep a watch out for a man with his name beginning with the letter "Z".'

I agreed. Dad didn't. 'And anyway, villagers don't normally carry handkerchiefs,' he said.

'Exactly! All the more reason to think that's a clue,' said Mom.

'But Dad, Mom,' I said urgently, 'you're missing the most vital *point* in this mystery.'

'And what is that?' asked Mom.

'There are a host of clues and suspects. But where's the mystery? Where are the ghosts? And if there are no ghosts, why are there these rumours?' I said.

'You're right!' Mom hopped up and down in excitement. 'We're here to find out *precisely* this. Gautam, where are the ghosts, eh! And if there are no ghosts, what's the mystery?'

'I know what you're getting at,' said Dad putting his hand up as if to ward her off, 'and I shan't allow it, okay?'

'What did you think I was going to say?' said Mom.

'I know you. You want to go to Saheb Bagan at night to see the dashed ghosts,' said Dad, 'and I shan't allow it, I tell you.'

'Why why why??? *I'm* not the kid here.'

That was so, so unfair. I point her in the right direction and now she blames me for something I can't help.

'Remember, Jiten begged you not to come? He said it was dangerous. *You* insisted. I've gone along with it long enough,' said Dad. 'It may be very very dangerous, Maya.'

'But you don't *know* that!' Mom looked at Dad, arms akimbo.

'Jiten said...'

'Pooh!' Mom waved away what Jiten said. 'We are documentary filmmakers. Where there's a mystery, there's definitely a dashed good documentary.'

'That old man also said that there might be ghosts, or there might be smugglers, or bandits or what have you. Even *he* warned us not to go there at night. Physical danger, he said, remember?'

Mom waved the old man away. 'He's just an old man. Naturally, he'd be spooked by such stories. Are you trying to tell me you're scared of a couple of two-bit ghosts or smugglers or what have you? I'm not saying we're going to *catch* them. We can go to *see* them. Silently.'

'Mom, Dad,' I had suddenly remembered the important thing, 'the old man was wearing floaters. *And* I think he was driving the jeep.'

Dad waved at me. 'Not now Andu.' He turned to Mom.

'Listen, Maya, be reasonable. You've got a kid...'

'So have you. It's your kid too...'

I decided to get out of there. I didn't want to know what percentage of me belonged to Dad and what percent to Mom. I'd heard this before. And anyway I knew Mom would win. She always does. I signaled to Kammu (who had so far been listening intently to all of us in silence) to come out with me.

As I swept the curtain aside and walked out of the room, I almost bumped into Jamirbhai. He staggered back a little and muttered something about tea being ready. How time flies when you're having an argument, I thought. I stalked towards the table, yelling, 'Mom, Dad, TEA!' But the table was empty. I turned around and glared at Jamirbhai. He quickly scuttled off saying something about 'getting the tea'.

It was a very uncomfortable tea. There was tea and bread and butter and Parle-G biscuits. I like tea. At home I'm never allowed tea.

I couldn't eat much because the lunch still lay heavy in my stomach. Dad and Mom glowered at each other across the table. I hurriedly finished my tea in a gulp, shoved the last bite of bread and butter in my mouth and with a muttered excuse, left the table. They didn't even notice.

Kammu gives me some advice

I made my way across the garden to the car where Kammu was just finishing his tea. He was leaning against the fender of the car, sipping his tea, while the empty, crumby plate of bread butter and biscuits lay balanced on the bonnet.

'Kammu,' I said, climbing on to the bonnet of the car, 'what do you think?'

Kammu finished his tea with a leisurely slurp. I looked down at him with envy. I had to gulp mine. I hadn't even tasted it properly.

'Kammu thinks we need torch,' he said, wiping his mouth with the back of his hand.

'Why?'

'You want to go Bhoot Bagan?'

'Ye-es. I suppose so.' I wasn't sure.

'Mummydaddy won't take you. They ask me to sleep in your room tonight. But you and I follow mummydaddy when they go.' Kammu nodded his head wisely at me. I stared at him.

'When did Dad ask you?'

'Not yet. But he will. Bet.' He opened his palm.

'No bet,' I said.

Kammu was right. Dad and Mom would go. I knew Mom would go. And Dad wouldn't let her go alone. And he wouldn't want to take me. So I'd be left alone in the Dak Bungalow with Kammu to guard me. I made up my mind. I'd rather go with Mom and Dad than stay here in this spooky place.

I clambered down from the bonnet. 'I'll go get my torch.'

'Not get. Keep ready.'

Dinner was again chicken and rice but it was a very silent meal. Dad looked preoccupied. Mom looked a little sheepish. She kept glancing at Dad and me, but wouldn't meet my eyes. After dinner, Mom stretched and stifled a yawn. 'It's been a long day,' she said, still avoiding my eyes, 'I think we should call it a day.' Dad muttered something and got up. I didn't say anything. I didn't know what to say.

After dinner I noticed Dad slipping away down the garden towards the car where Kammu was probably having his dinner. He's gone to talk to Kammu, I thought. While I was getting ready for bed, I heard a soft, low whistle from the garden. I crept out to the veranda and looked around. Kammu detached himself from the shadow of some bushes and came up to the veranda.

'They go midnight. Don't want you scare. So ask me to sleep in your room. So you not suspect they go.'

I felt a little mad. They didn't want me go, so they had asked Kammu to come to my room at midnight with his roll of bedding and sleep there. It was unfair.

Was I a part of the team or not? They could have at least *told* me. At first I had been feeling a little bad about disobeying them, but now I felt no qualms at all.

'Bring biscuit,' said Kammu before melting away into the shadows of the garden, 'Will be hungry at night.'

The Locked Door

Kammu knocked on my door at precisely 11.45 pm. I was lying on my bed, fully dressed, trying to fight sleep.

I got up with a jump and rushed to open the door. I turned the handle. It wouldn't budge. Kammu had locked me in, the silly fellow! Kammu knocked again, 'Hello, hello, should leave before daddymummy. Are you sleep?'

'Kammu,' I whispered urgently from this side of the door. 'Unbolt the door, silly. You've locked me in.'

'What?' Kammu rattled the doorknob. I gritted my teeth. He was making such a racket that it was a wonder my parents weren't here already.

'Kammu,' I raised my voice. 'Shut up and listen.'

I am normally never rude to people. Mom would kill me. But this time I just *had* to make him listen.

Kammu listened. There was shocked silence on the other side.

'Kammu, you've locked me in. Unlock the door.'

I heard the bolt being pushed back. Kammu peered inside. He looked indignant. 'You say shuddup.'

I 'sorried' him but also told him that he shouldn't have knocked so hard. That had locked the door from outside. 'I never,' said Kammu, indignantly. He pointed at his face. 'I look stupid to you?' he asked. I stopped to think. That made him madder still and I had to 'sorry' him some more before he calmed down. Then we arranged one bolster on the bed, and a pillow and another bolster on the floor, covered them up to look like me and Kammu, and slipped out into the night. All this had taken some time, and the glowing green dial of my watch told me that it was midnight as we crept out of the Dak Bungalow gates.

'I hope we don't bump into Mom and Dad,' I whispered to Kammu as we walked, hugging the hedges at the side of the road.

'They sleep maybe,' Kammu whispered back. 'I no see them come out. Door closed.'

The night was cool and the sky looked soft and hung very low over our heads. It had thousands of stars in it, and each one of them looked bright and shiny, like well-polished beautiful crystals. Millions of dancing fireflies lit up the hedges in front of us.

After a while, I took out some biscuits from my bag and we walked along, munching in silence. Strangely enough, I was loving this silent walk along the empty road, and wasn't thinking about Saheb Bagan or anything else at all.

I didn't even realise when we crossed the marketplace, everything was so peaceful. No humans, no cats, no dogs, no rabbits, mice or hedgehogs, no owls—there was no sign of any living thing. And there was absolutely no sound, except for the cicadas.

Adventure in the darkness

Suddenly, Kammu clutched hard at my arm.

'Side, side, hide, quick!' he breathed into my ear, pushing me against the hedge at the side of the road. I flattened myself against it and tried to pretend I was a bush or something. I was just in time. A truck whooshed by, just inches from us, throwing dust on our faces. Its headlights were switched off, so I hadn't noticed it coming. And it made no sound. No rattling or clanking noises that trucks normally make. It drove by us, absolutely silently, a dark shape, towards Saheb Bagan.

'Run, Kammu,' I whispered into his ear as I

began running after the truck. We were only about a hundred yards or so from the gates of Saheb Bagan. I hadn't realised that we were so close. 'Why we run?' Kammu breathed as we trotted silently after the truck. 'Because someone will have to open the gates for the truck to enter, silly. We might be able to slip in behind it. Otherwise we'll have to climb the wall, and that's going to be a pain.'

The truck began to slow down as it neared the gates. And then I got a shock. The whole gate began to slide sideways silently. I mean, I had expected someone to be standing at the gate, opening those huge locks, unwinding the chains and then pushing open the gate from the middle for the truck to enter. But the huge gate slid sideways, locks and chains and all, slowly creating an opening for the truck to pass.

'I never see gate open like that,' muttered Kammu, wide eyed.

'Nor have I,' I said, giving Kammu a push. We sidled inside slowly after the truck, and crouched behind a couple of bushes as the truck drove away down the driveway. The gate slowly slid back into place, and stood there as before, locks and chains in place, looking just like any other ordinary, old, rusty gate.

Something clicked in my mind. 'I know,' I said,

snapping my fingers, 'I should have realised it before, there's no mud anywhere around. The ground is dry. So how did the locks get muddy? You see, Kammu, they were pretend locks. They were new, and someone had to make them seem old. They couldn't make the locks rust fast, so they coated them with mud to make them look old.'

Kammu slowly nodded. 'But why pretend?' he said.

'Because if you wrap chains around the middle of a gate and put locks on it, people won't notice that the gate opens sideways. They will think that it's like any ordinary gate which opens from the middle. They'll see that it's locked and won't try to open it. Especially if you design the gate so that it looks like it opens from the middle.' I ran to the side of the gate and peered at the wall beside it in excitement. 'I bet this gate is easy to open. I bet whoever made it couldn't always keep it locked and so he made it *look* locked to keep out people. I bet the gang knows how to open this gate.'

'Which gang?'

'THE gang, Kammu, the gang which comes in this truck to do whatever it has to do,' I said, impatiently, feeling along the sides of the wall for any switch or button or whatever which would open the gate.

Kamu tugged at my sleeve. 'Why not open gate later? Right now see bhootbungalow.'

I stopped my fumbling. 'Good idea. Let's take a look at the bungalow. Let's also take a look at the truck.'

We turned to walk down the driveway towards the bungalow. We walked softly and kept right at the edge of the path, pressing ourselves as much into the bushes as possible. As we turned a corner in the driveway, the Bhoot Bungalow loomed up before us, dark and silent. Not a chink of light glowed through its shuttered doors and windows.

I turned to Kammu, 'Do you think the truck is parked somewhere behind the bungalow?' I whispered.

In reply, Kammu clutched hard at my tee shirt and breathed into my face. 'What that?'

'What's what?' I said, turning around impatiently. And I froze in horror.

Something weird was happening. I could see a sort of dim greenish glow lighting up the front of the bungalow. It grew brighter and now I could see a greenish phosphorescent smoke like thing glowing, coiling and uncoiling itself, now glowing dimmer, now brighter. It was like a glowing green cloud on the ground along the façade of the bungalow. The bungalow looked as if it was suspended in the cloud a little above the ground. I hung on to Kammu's arm tightly, shivering in fear.

After a while, the green cloud seemed to dim and fade away. I breathed.

'Look, there,' Kammu clutched at me again. The front door of the bungalow had opened silently. A dim green glow came from within. The green glow slowly grew stronger and again the smoke started forming, coiling around and about silently. It was like an evil cloud, covering the door of the house. And this time, through the green cloud, we could see something else. A huge furry creature, its fur glowing green, was coming right at us. It wasn't really walking but was half limping, half dragging itself towards us. It was dragging itself down the stairs, glowing eerily green, the cloud around it making it seem like it was half suspended above the ground, like the house.

My heart was hammering so loudly, I think even that creature could hear. The blood was in my head. 'Run, Kammu,' I tried to shout, but what came out was a croak. Without another word, we turned and ran. Hand in hand, we ran, crashing through the bushes, Kammu dragging me along behind him. We ran across the garden, not looking back, hearing the sound of our ragged breathing, and still seeing that unearthly creature in our mind's eye.

We rushed headlong towards the gate and I tried to tug at Kammu's hand to ask him to slow down, we had to find the button to open the gate, but he rushed on, and to my utter horror I saw the gate sliding open sideways, silently, smoothly, as we neared it. It was as if the gate had sensed that someone wanted to go out and had opened obligingly.

We dashed out into the night and I turned to watch the gate slide shut behind us. We didn't stop running for miles afterward.

When we reached our Dak Bungalow, Kammu made me 'God Promise' not to tell daddymummy what had happened tonight, because he said that if they found out that Kammu had taken me into danger instead of guarding me like he was supposed to, he would lose his job and his whole family would starve to death. I was so tired I would have agreed to anything by then. So I nodded.

I huddled under my bedclothes, shivering as I thought of that creature from hell coming out of the Bhoot Bungalow at us before falling asleep. I had terrible dreams of gates opening and shutting and green clouds chasing me all across the garden of Bhoot Bagan.

The Invitation

The next morning, I wasn't feeling happy at all. I was sleepy, my legs ached and I was racked with guilt. I couldn't look Mom and Dad in the eye though they didn't seem to notice. They were hopping mad at something. At first I thought that they had discovered my nocturnal escapade, and my heart sank. But when Mom asked me, 'Andu, did you lock us in last night?' I was so relieved, I could look at her in the eye and honestly and fervently deny it.

'Then who did?' She demanded, stirring her tea so violently, that some of it splashed onto the table. 'I don't know Mom,' I answered wearily, and she glared at me across the table.

I forgot about it soon after, when, just as we were finishing breakfast, Jamirbhai handed a rather large, wrinkled brown paper envelope to Dad.

'Babu,' he said, rudely thrusting it at Dad, 'From Deputy DM's bungalow.' Craning my neck over Dad's shoulder, I read.

To

Mr. & Mrs. Choudhuri and family

This is to invite your esteemed selves to a humble dinner party I am holding in your honour. I shall be grateful if you would attend dinner in my humble abode tonight at 8.00 pm in the night. My humble abode shall be elevated by the presence of your esteemed selves.

Thanking You
Your Humble Servant
Baidyanath Chatterjee
(Deputy District Magistrate)

'It'll be rude not to go,' said Dad handing the envelope to Mom.

'But we're supposed to go to...' hissed Mom fiercely at Dad and glancing furtively at me.

'I know. But how can we refuse?' Dad frowned. 'We can always go after the dinner party. After all, in the villages, people go to bed early. I'm sure we can get back here by eleven. That will give us plenty of time to get ready for the...eh...never mind."

'If I could only get my hands on the fellow who locked our door,' fumed Mom. 'I wanted to go to, you know, *there*, last night.' She again glanced at me out of the corner of her eyes.

'I know, I know,' said Dad, soothingly. 'But someone locked us in our bedroom, and we couldn't. So, tonight after coming back from dinner, I'll stand guard outside our room while you get ready for the, uh, going *there*,' finished Dad in a whisper.

They thought I didn't know about their plan to visit Saheb Bagan at night. I wished that I really hadn't known. I wished that I hadn't gone there last night. I wished I was as innocent as they thought I was. I was the worst criminal and liar and knave and villain in the world. I felt miserable. I got up and left the table. Also, I badly wanted to sleep.

That Evening

In the evening, I woke up from my nap feeling refreshed, but as guilty as ever. I promised myself that I would confess as soon I was able to convince Kammu that it wasn't his fault and that he wouldn't be fired. This made me feel better, and I hung around the Dak Bungalow the rest of the day messing about almost happily.

As soon as it was getting dark, we left for the Deputy District Magistrate's house. As the car lurched along the road, I clicked pictures of the passing scenery with my camera.

Suddenly it occurred to me that I could have taken it along with me last night. I could have taken pictures of that evil green thing. And they would have bought it and published it in all the magazines across the world. 'THE FIRST EVER PICTURE OF A SUPERNATURAL BEING!' the headlines would scream and my name as photographer would be underneath it and I would be famous and make lots of money and would never have to go to school. Instead I could go off to Antarctica and click more photos and make more money...

BLAM!

My brain jumped out of my skull.

Kammu turned around. 'Not worry. Tyre gone puncture.'

I noticed that we had reached the marketplace by then.

In the fading light of dusk, the marketplace looked very different from the quaint touristy picture it made during the day. Now the wicks of the little oil lamps made from the green coconut hair oil tins glimmered in the small makeshift stalls. Dim shadows gathered the darkness to themselves and grew from grey to black under the trees. The people looked dark and ghostly and the glow worms danced their starry green dances wherever the shadows were thickest. Some of the bigger stalls had hurricane lamps and as Kammu pulled the car over to one side, I noticed that the Riceplate Man's restaurant and the cycle repair shop were both closed. The wooden doors and windows were shut and no light gleamed through their ill-fitting frames. Hmmm...so no one was inside, I gathered. The darkness made me remember last night, and I began to feel very uneasy.

Kammu had started rummaging for the stepney and jack behind the car when I came out of my blue funk and saw that both Dad and Mom were not in the car. I hastily scrambled out. After last night I didn't want to be left alone in the darkness, not for one moment.

We had stopped in front of a small chicken shop. I hadn't noticed it in the morning because it was almost hidden behind a huge peepal tree. Now the hurricane lamp gave the shop a definition and separated it from the deep cool shade of the tree.

I hurried up to my parents who were standing at the entrance to the chicken shop. The cassette shop suddenly spilled out a Hindi film song and it sounded loud and very out of place in the melancholy night air.

'Is there a chai shop nearby,' I heard Dad asking as I came near. He was speaking to the owner of the chicken shop. I peeked into the shop and immediately wished I hadn't. The air inside the poky little shop was thick with the smell of chicken and dried blood. It was untidy and messy with feathers and chicken claws and other bloody stuff littered all over the place. The sawn off piece of wooden log used for cutting the chickens looked as if it had never been cleaned. I hastily withdrew my head and looked at the Chicken Man and again wished I hadn't. He was wearing a blood spattered ganji and a green check lungi and scratching his bald head with a hand which had blood encrusted on its knuckles. I could see it even in the dim light. He probably never washed. I shuddered.

'There is the rice plate shop which is also a chai shop but today...'

'It is closed,' Dad finished the sentence the Chicken Man had started. 'I noticed. Any other?'

The Chicken Man looked thoughtfully at Dad. Then suddenly he smiled. I wish he hadn't. His teeth were stained red with pan juice and they stuck out under his fleshy glistening gums like an evil alien's in all directions.

'Please don't mind babu, can I ask you a question?'

Dad looked surprised. 'Yes?'

'Are you the party from Kolkata staying at the Dak Bungalow?'

'Yes.' Dad was again into his milk-from-cheese act. The man would have to drag facts out of him.

'How do you know?' asked Mom.

I groaned. 'Moooom...' This was an Indian village, for god's sake. We had shot here in the morning. *Everybody* knew who we were and where we were staying, down to the last stray dog in the marketplace. But what the Chicken Man said next pulled me up short.

'Jamir is buying extra chickens now. Yesterday and today he bought two extra chickens.' And he grinned. I shut my eyes to block out the sight of his stained teeth. 'Usually he buys only two,' I opened my eyes.

'Usually, when there is no one staying at the Dak Bungalow, he buys two chickens?' I couldn't help asking.

The Chicken Man's head bobbed up and down. He was nodding. 'He is my best customer babu. Daily two chickens. Now you come, he buys four. I am the only Muslim chicken shop here. Rehman's Chicken Shop.' He proudly pointed at the rickety tin board nailed on top of the door of his shop. In the middle of the board was drawn a chicken which looked like a cross between a largish swan and a goose, with REHMAN written in Bengali in green letters all across the board under the bird. It looked as if the bird was called Rehman.

But my mind was still on Jamirbhai's extra-ordinary talent. 'What an appetite!' I marveled. 'He doesn't look like he eats two chickens a day.'

'Yeah,' Mom nodded. 'He looks like a scrawny bit of chicken himself.'

'Yeah,' Dad sighed. 'Hidden depths. Who would have suspected the old man to have so much chicken in him?' Mom and Dad looked at each other and laughed.

Dad sighed and looked at his watch. 'I hope we aren't getting late. In villages people usually dine and go to bed pretty early.'

'Where do you want to go?' Dad had spoken the last sentence in Bengali, so Rehman had understood.

'The Deputy Magistrate's bungalow.'

'Deputy's bungalow? You can go there across rice fields. Ten minutes,' said Rehman.

'Thank you, but no. I'm not walking across paddy fields in the dark.' Mom shook her head at Dad.

'Tyre change!' announced Kammu.

'Thank God!' sighed Dad as we hurriedly piled into the car.

'Mom,' I said after a minute or two of silence after the car had started moving. 'Did you notice the Chicken Man's...'

Mom shuddered. 'I don't even want to think about it. Your Dad chooses the most extraordinary people to talk to.'

'That's completely unfair!' protested Dad. 'Who found out that Jamir eats two chickens a day?'

Mom looked smug. 'I have a talent for finding out things. Can I help that?' She raised her eyebrows at Dad.

Then a very surprising thing happened. Suddenly Kammu spoke up. 'Jamir no eat chicken.

Doctor said no meat. Jamir eat no chicken no mutton no egg. Only dal rice and boiled vegetables. He says his sister kill him if he eat meat.'

'Then he must be buying it for his sister,' I said. Kammu glanced at me witheringly through the rear view mirror, 'or...his family or something...' I trailed off unconvincingly.

'Jamir sister across border. In Bangladesh. No other family. No other job. Only caretaker of dak-bungalow. Any case can't have two chicken a day in chickenfeed salary.' Kammu chortled at his own joke.

We arrived at the Deputy DM's bungalow in pin-drop silence.

Mr. Deputy's Bungalow

Our 'esteemed' selves gazed upon the 'humble abode' in awe. The bungalow looked like a ghastly little mini palace. It had verandas and strange cupola like shapes sticking out in all directions. Even in the darkness I could make out that it was a terrible shade of crazy pink. A uniformed manservant opened the large ornately decorated gates and we swept up the drive to the house.

'Mom,' I said, as the car stopped in front of the main door, 'your mouth is open.'

Mom closed her mouth, swallowed and asked Dad in a whisper, 'Is this his official residence?'

'Of course not. Have you ever seen government quarters which look like this? It's his own house.'

Mr. Deputy Magistrate himself came out to the front door to welcome us. He looked like a character out of a Bengali comic book. He was short and fat and his face was completely round. He was bald except for a few strands of hair, which he had neatly brushed across his gleaming baldness in a vain attempt to cover it. He was wearing a starched kurta and crisply pleated dhoti, and diamond studded gold buttons gleamed on his hairy chest. I had only seen people wearing clothes like this at weddings or thread ceremonies.

'*Nomoshkar, Nomoshkar*!!' he shouted. 'So this is the famous Choudhuri family.' He ushered us in fussily, shouting into Dad's ear that he was happy we had graced his 'humble abode' and that it had 'elevated' his prestige to have us accept his dinner invitation. Dad winced. Mom smiled at him mischievously. Dad glared at her.

Several uniformed servants hovered around as Mr. Deputy led us across the elaborately decorated hall to the sitting room. 'This is the HALL,' he yelled at us as we gaped at the pink velvet curtains and the thick rose red carpet on the floor. Even the lights had pink shades, I noticed, feeling a little unreal. He took us to a pink curtained door at the far end of the hall and sweeping the curtain aside, he announced, 'and this is...'

'THE SITTING ROOM!' I screamed, beaming at him. Mr. Deputy looked a little taken aback while I heard Mom stifle a giggle behind me. The sitting room was also a poem in pink with two large pink sofas and several pink overstuffed chairs.

We were introduced to a pale faced man sitting in the corner of one of the huge pink sofas. who was trying to look as if he wasn't there. He was apparently a bosom friend of our host and was called Mr. Das and was supposed to be a *thekedar* by profession. He got up when introductions were being made and bowed jerkily at the coffee table.

'What's a *thekedar* Mom,' I muttered while our host tried to decide our seating arrangements.

'Cuts trees in forests on government contracts' was her cryptic explanation as Deputy DM shouted at her from across the room to 'take the sofa, PLEASE!'

I decided I'd ask for explanations later.

Mr. Das was as different from our host as night from day. Our host shouted, Das whispered. Our host was the life and soul of the party, Das faded into the background like an insubstantial ghost. Our host's rollicking laughter told us that he hadn't a care in the world, while Das sat and worried, chewing his lower lip and glancing furtively at his watch watched his feet. When you spoke to him, he would consider the leg of the coffee table thoughtfully and then answer your right shoe.

Five minutes into the conversation and soft drinks, when my ears were beginning to feel numb, a servant entered the room and tentatively approached Mr. Deputy DM. He bent down and whispered something into his ears and at once his face became blank. It was as if someone had taken a sponge and wiped off all the joy and bonhomie from his face. He looked at us with his expressionless face which made me shiver. He suddenly looked scary. Then he made a hurried excuse and left the room. Dad and Mom began to talk together in low voices. Das was sitting in his corner, sunk in some deep dark thoughts of his own. I silently got up and went out of the room. I let the curtain fall back behind me as I looked at the pink expanse of hallway in front. I was debating which way to go, when I saw a faint shadow move under a door at the opposite end of the hall. Someone was in there.

I ran across the hall to the door as quietly as I could and put my ear to the door. The door hadn't latched properly and it swung open silently. It was the study. There was a desk facing the door and our host was sitting on a chair facing the door. A man was standing with his back to me, and facing Mr. Deputy. There was something familiar about the man though I could not immediately place him.

'You don't know me! How many times have I got to tell you that?' Mr. Deputy's voice was a low animal snarl, and now he was looking quite unlike the Bengali comic book character that he had reminded me of initially. His face was twisted in a scowl and his eyes glittered with an evil light. His mouth was flecked with spittle. He was obviously in a towering rage.

'But Babu...' the voice was low, almost a whisper, but the hair on the back of my neck stood up. It was Jamirbhai! What was he doing here? My mind began buzzing again. I shook my head to clear it and tried to concentrate on what he was saying. 'But Babu, they spoke to Rehman. When they left, I asked him what he had said. He said he told them I buy chickens from his shop.'

Who was Jamirbhai talking about? Who spoke to Rehman? With a thrill of fear I realised that he was talking about us. That meant that Jamirbhai had somehow seen us in Rehman's chicken shop. Had he been following us?

'Idiot! You've risked everything we are working for to come and tell me this! I shall wring your neck!'

Mr. Deputy's voice was more snarly and animal like if possible.

'Not only because of that Babu, but what I heard them say made me feel that they will try and go to the bagan again tonight.'

And *that* meant that Jamirbhai was deliberately eavesdropping on us in the morning. And what did he mean by 'again'? Did that mean he knew someone had gone to the bagan last night? Was Jamirbhai keeping track of all our movements? I felt angry. The filthy spy!

'Go to the bagan again tonight! We must prevent them at all cost. Bloody pests!' He swore.

Jamirbhai wrung his hands. 'What should I do?' he wailed, 'if anything happens to me, what will my sister do?'

'Idiot! What can happen to you? If they know anything at all, they know that you eat a lot of chicken. That's not a crime! And the boy won't dare say a word to his parents about last night. He's too scared. What we have to think about is how to stop them from going to the bagan again tonight. There may be grave danger.' My heart began a slow, painful *thump...thump...thump...*I was sweating. I raised my hand to wipe the sweat on my forehead, and suddenly realised that I was still holding my camera. I don't know what happened to me then.

Something went 'phut' in my brain, and I became wild. I quickly changed the button to low light mode, switched off the flash and raised the camera. As if waiting for my signal, Jamirbhai half turned his face and I pressed the button. The 'wheeerrclick' sounded loud in the silence and both of them froze. I swiftly darted behind the long velvet curtains of another closed door to my right. There was silence for a while and then I heard the study door being flung open and our host's voice shouting for the servants. I didn't dare breathe. If they found me, I would be *kheema*. I just knew it. My heart was bursting. I was suffocating behind the curtains, I would be found any minute. The Deputy's evil expression in the study danced before my eyes. 'Fool! Fool!! Fool!!!' I told myself and sagged against the door. And almost lost my balance and fell. The rule in this house seemed to be that latches didn't latch properly. This door was also ajar, and I had almost fallen on my bum inside the room. I looked around and almost fainted with relief. It was a bathroom. A pink bathroom, but a bathroom. I quickly got up and latched the door from inside. Outside I could hear the sounds of the search increasing. The servants were flinging open all the doors around the hall one by one and inspecting the rooms. I could hear my parents' voices. They had also heard the commotion and come out into the hall. And they had realised that I was missing. Someone hammered on my door and the noise almost took my skull off. I jumped back from the door rubbing my ear and made my voice sound irritable. 'Who is it? Go away! I have a bad tummy.'

Then I heard Mom's voice. She knocked on the door. 'Andu, are you there? Are you alright? Apparently some smalltime thief tried to get inside the house through a window or something...you're sure you're ok?'

'I'm OK Mom. I'm just...I just have a slightly bad tummy.' I hurriedly thrust the camera into one of the many pockets of my cargo pants, washed my hands in the basin with a lot of splashy noises and then wiped my hands and came out. To be greeted by the entire household standing around in a half circle outside the bathroom door staring at me.

'Thank god you're all right,' said Mom rushing at me.

'Mom,' I said, slightly irritated, 'it's not cholera, for god's sake.'

'Mr. Chatterjee seemed to have a notion that the thief was holding you hostage or something in the bathroom.'

'What thief?' I asked innocently. 'I just ate something a little nasty,' and out of sheer mischief, added, 'maybe it was Jamirbhai's chicken.' Out of the corner of my eyes I noticed Mr. Deputy start and glance sharply at me. I looked at him and shouted, 'Chatterjeekaku, you have a lovely bathroom!' Mr. Deputy's expression changed. In an instant he again became the slightly stupid comic book Bengali bridegroom. He shouted back at us and asked us to come back to the sitting room again since the thief business was obviously a false alarm.

Jamirbhai must have slipped away before Mr. Deputy had raised the alarm. And that had also given me enough time to hide. Phew!

Dinner was a disaster. I was bursting to tell Mom and Dad what I had overheard. I wanted to tell them about last night too. I wanted to finish off everything quickly and go back to the Dak Bungalow. And then I wanted Dad and me to go visit Saheb Bagan again. I was now almost sure that that 'thing' yesterday was no ghost. It was something meant to scare us away. Dad would find out. He wouldn't be afraid, I was sure.

My brain was churning. Why didn't Mr. Deputy want us to go there tonight? What was the 'grave danger' lurking in Saheb Bagan? I was dying to find out. I hardly tasted what I ate. Mom got irritated with me after sometime. 'Stop stuffing your face like that!' She hissed at me across the table. 'No wonder you've got a bad tummy. And stop fidgeting. You're acting like you've got ants in your pants.'

I tried to go slow from then on, but it was difficult to sit still. In his turn, Mr. Deputy dragged out the dinner for as long as possible. I realised that he was trying to delay us. He was witty, he cracked jokes, he narrated funny incidents, but after a while I realised that even he was getting tired. He wasn't shouting loudly enough, and his stories sounded forced and weren't funny anymore. But finally, dinner was over. The last course was *payesh*. I didn't want it. I don't like sweets much. Even Mom and Dad don't. We refused. And Mr. Deputy went crazy. He told us how he had it especially made for us. He had himself selected the finest of rice and the best of *nolen gur*. You should have heard him. He begged. He pleaded. He looked ready to cry. Mom and Dad looked at each other. I knew they were going to give in. They are polite people. They get embarrassed easily. And I was right. They pulled the bowls of *payesh* towards them and began to eat. I watched, suddenly feeling uneasy. 'It tastes peculiar,' mouthed Mom to Dad. Dad shrugged.

'Your boy not eating?' suddenly Mr. Deputy shouted, beaming at my parents.

'No,' I said stubbornly. 'My tummy feels strange.' And to stop further argument, I threatened, 'I'm going to throw up if I eat anything else.'

Mom and Dad looked at me anxiously. I shook

my head at them. I wanted to tell them not to eat the *payesh* but I knew they wouldn't understand what I was trying to say. My instincts were telling me that something was wrong. I felt Mr. Deputy glaring at me. I turned to look at him. I caught a glimpse of his face twisted in a snarl of rage before he hastily smoothened it back again into its usual jolly look. I hated him then and I felt terribly scared.

There was something happening here that I couldn't understand. And couldn't stop. It was as if a river had burst its banks and we were being swept along with it. And I knew that there were rapids ahead and I couldn't warn anyone. No one would hear me if I shouted, the sound of the rushing water was so loud. I felt so totally helpless.

The Gari Story

Dinner was finally over and I heaved a sigh of relief. We could finally go now. Mr. Deputy couldn't keep us at his house any longer, I thought. But I was so wrong. As we were beginning to say our goodbyes, Kammu came rushing into the room.

'Sir! *Gari* won't start!'

'What!' exclaimed Dad. 'What wrong with it now? Another puncture?'

'No puncture. It won't *start*.'

'So what's wrong?' asked Dad trying to stifle a yawn.

'Donno. Have to call mechanic in the morning.'

Kammu generally does the small scale repairs on our car himself. If he had to call a mechanic then what was wrong with our car was not a minor matter. Dad also realised that.

'Oh god!' he said, stifling another yawn, 'Kammu, how do we go home then? It's past midnight.'

'I can't walk,' said Mom slumping into a chair and yawning widely. 'I'm really sleepy. Funny, it's only twelvish. Must be all this fresh country air. Remember how sleepy Andubabu was this morning?'

'Dad,' I said firmly. Dad looked at me kind of blearily, I thought. 'Can't we go in one of Chatterjeekaku's cars?' To call this villain Chatterjeekaku stuck in my throat, but I had no option. Appearances had to be kept.

Mr. Deputy smiled silkily at me. 'Smart boy. But unfortunately, my dear, not smart enough.' His eyes glittered at me. 'Both my cars have gone for servicing. So your only option is to spend the night here, in my house, as my guests. I shall be glad to accommodate you.'

I knew then that he knew that I knew. He had given my parents something to make them feel sleepy, so they wouldn't protest much when he offered them his hospitality for the night. And he also had them, and me in a place where he could keep an eye on us so that we wouldn't interfere with whatever he had going on at Saheb Bagan that night.

That thought made me boil with rage as I lay on one of Mr. Deputy's beds in one of his many guestrooms, listening to the deep, rasping breathing of my parents. I had insisted on sharing a room with them and Mr. Deputy had given us a large room with a separate cot for me.

'The room has an attached bathroom,' pointed out Mr. Deputy to me, 'so you won't need to go out at night. Understand, smart boy?' He had almost hissed the last words at me, and I felt myself recoil in horror.

After a while, I got out of bed and went to the door. I tried to open it, but the latch wouldn't turn. I wasn't surprised. I had known that they would lock us in, since I had refused to eat the *payesh* and that man didn't trust me not to go wandering about on my own.

I threw myself back into my cot and tried to go to sleep. And the last thing I heard before I fell asleep was Mr. Deputy's voice hissing in my ear, 'Smart boy. But unfortunately, my dear, not smart enough.'

Evil in the Morning

Mom and Dad absolutely refused to believe me the next morning when I told them that their *payesh* had been spiked and we had been locked in our bedrooms the whole night. 'It was the fresh country air and the heavy dinner. Lethal combination,' they insisted, yawning widely. 'We were locked in *last* night. At the Dak Bungalow. Why would Chatterjee want to lock us up in his house?'

'To stop you from going to Saheb Bagan at night,' I said.

'Nonsense. What has he got to do with Saheb Bagan. He's like a cartoon character,' said Mom waving her hand dismissively.

'There are lots of evil cartoon characters,' I insisted.

'How would he know we were about to go?' asked Mom.

'Jamirbhai told him last night. He came to meet him. Look.' I pressed the preview button in my camera and showed them the photo I had taken. It didn't look so menacing in the morning light. In the photo both Jamirbhai and the Deputy were looking in the general direction of the camera, and both looked kind of startled. It was also slightly out of focus.

I also told them that I had heard someone unlocking the latch of the door of our room very quietly at about six in the morning. I had woken up at the sound with a jump.

I had been jumpy throughout the night. You would be too, if your parents had been drugged.

They looked at me disbelievingly. 'It's all right Andu,' Mom said, ruffling my hair. 'We know you didn't like the deputy. And it's natural for Jamir to know him. Both of them live in the same village, for god's sake. There might have been any number of reasons why Jamir might want to meet him. But it's absurd to suggest that everyone in this village is hell bent on stopping us from going to Saheb Bagan. And so hell bent that they'd go to absurd lengths such as doping our food! This is not the Middle Ages. People don't do these kinds of things anymore.' She hugged me gently. 'Your imagination does get the better of you at times, Andu.'

I immediately made up my mind not to tell them about the green thing I had seen the other night. And about the clouds and mist. She didn't believe me now, she'd think I had gone nuts if she heard about all that.

'In this age what do you think they do?' I asked Mom gruffly.

'They threaten you with a gun. Or they bump

you off. Or...'

'Okay okay Maya,' interrupted Dad, 'I think he gets the point. Let's not become too gory here.'

Mom winked at me and turned to Dad. 'By the way, where *is* the deputy?' she asked.

'He sent his apologies through a servant. Urgent business in office. Had to leave early. Sorry but hope esteemed guests had good night,' said Dad getting into the car. Mom laughed. 'I had pink dreams,' she said.

I gave up. I decided I wouldn't tell them a thing from now on. My conscience was clear. I had tried to tell. They didn't believe. My duty was done.

The car started sweetly at the first turn of the key. Kammu was a little surprised, but relieved. 'Why?' I asked him. 'Why wouldn't the car start last night and how come it starts this morning without a whimper?'

'I don't question good luck,' Kammu told me severely, rubbing his eyes. He had spent the night in the servants' quarters. 'Very comfortable,' he had told me approvingly.

'You should.' I was equally severe. 'One should always know the reason why.'

'You know why you born?' he asked.

I was irritated. 'I don't think my being born was such a good idea,' I grumbled.

'Do not say such things. You insult Allah. You insult daddymummy. You insult me. You don't know your goodluck.' Kammu was being his preachy avatar and I wasn't in the mood for being preached. So I just stuck my tongue out at him and subsided into my seat. No one was willing to see the scientific evidence of car tampering which was right in front of their eyes. No one could see the evil that was all around us. I shivered from the cool morning air coming in through the open window of the car. Goodluck...eh?

I wished that daddymummy had been there at the Saheb Bagan with us when that green thing came out. They would then have believed that there was Evil at work around us. I hadn't been able to figure out yet what Evil was actually working at, but I would, and soon, I vowed, rubbing the goosebumps on my arms.

Murder!

When we reached the Dak Bungalow, Mom went straight up to her room. After five seconds she came out looking completely weird. She was kind of swaying. As if the ground was like a heaving sea and she couldn't figure where to step. 'G a u t a m...' she croaked in a strange, broken sort of voice. Dad rushed up the stairs into their bedroom. I followed. I was alarmed because she sounded so strange and far away. She waved at me to stay back. 'Gautam...no Andu, he mustn't see...' and she suddenly crumpled up from the middle as if her backbone had turned to jelly. Dad caught her before she fell to the ground and stuffed her into one of the chairs in the veranda, where she lolled like a rag doll. And then he turned to me. 'Look after her, Andu,' he said in a tight sort of voice, 'I must see...' and he rushed towards their room.

'Mom,' I shouted, shaking her, scared at the way her head was flopping about. 'What's wrong with you? Wake up!'

'She fainted,' said Kammu's voice in my ear. 'Like heroine in *filum*.'

'What should I do, Kammu?' I was desperate. Dad had asked me to look after her. I didn't know the first thing about sick people. Or people who fainted. It was alright in a movie. But in real life, it scared me so, that I had become iceman. Completely frozen. My feet wouldn't move, my brain couldn't think.

'Here,' Kammu handed me something. I looked down at it. It was a jug. Full of water.

'What do I do with it?' I asked stupidly.

'Drink it,' Kammu sounded sarcastic. I frowned.

He sighed. 'Throw it on her face.' And when I still didn't react, because my brain was taking time to figure out what he was saying, he said, 'like in *filum*.'

I threw the water on her face. I must have thrown it really hard because the next thing I heard was her gasping and sputtering. I then heard her voice. 'Whatdyuu mean by wetting me like this, Andu?' And I saw Mom frowning up at me crossly, water dripping down her front.

And something went click in my brain and everything became all right again. I then did something that I'd never ever thought of doing. I threw myself at her with a howl. 'Mom Mom Mom... you scared me.' I clung to her, shivering. Everything suddenly seemed too much for me to handle. It didn't matter that the front of my tee shirt was getting damp. 'I thought you were dead!'

'Not dead, not likely!' she said, hugging me back. 'It's just that I've never seen a dead body before. I sort of...um...freaked.'

'Dead body?' I drew back and stared at her. 'Whose dead body?'

'Haru Tantrik,' I heard Kammu say behind me. 'Stabbed with knife. Lots of blood. Come, see.'

'No no no,' Mom cried, trying to pull me back. 'It's horrible. All that blood,' and she shuddered.

'Like in the *filums*,' said Kammu with a lot of

satisfaction in his voice. 'Murder.'

After that I just *had* to go and see.

Haru Tantrik was lying on his stomach, arms spread out on the floor. I couldn't see his face, as it was turned away from the door. Blood had seeped out of his front and had created a dark pool around his chest. It reminded me of the iron tonic Mom used to give me last year. I had once spilled a lot of it on the floor, and it looked just like this. Haru's beard was matted in it.

As I looked down at him, I wondered why this man had come here, to the bungalow. Had he come to harm us? Or to help us? And did he know that coming to the bungalow was the last thing he would be doing in his life? What kind of a man had he been? What had he felt as he was dying? Had he known he was dying?

My head suddenly felt swimmy. I felt a hard grip on my arm. 'Here, you no behave like heroine, eh?' said Kammu at my elbow. Hearing his voice in my ear brought me back to the room.

'See, he looking at man who kill him,' said Kammu.

'That means he was facing the murderer,' I said, making my voice sound strong and unaffected. 'That means he must have known the murderer.'

I suddenly saw something clutched in Haru's outstretched right hand. Something skin coloured.

Something which looked like a thin membrane. I gingerly stepped across Haru's body and prised it open from his fingers.

'You no touch crime things,' Kammu scolded.

'I don't care,' I said, turning to go. I had had enough of the murder scene. 'Come see what I got. You'll find it interesting.'

After that it was chaos. The police came. Dad had called them. Kammu went off somewhere before I could talk to him. The Deputy DM came and flapped his fat hand at everyone. I overheard words like 'murder' and 'crime' and 'immediate action'. Curious villagers came. Men, women and children buzzed around the place like flies, as the news spread. The police tried to keep them away and failed. So more police came. Someone came to take photos of the dead man. Faces and voices hurried past me and Mom while we sat on the chairs in the veranda of the Dak Bungalow trying to keep out of everyone's way. Someone handed us glasses of tea. A man started to sell peanuts to the crowd collected outside the gate.

More people turned up. Someone spread a sheet of plastic on the side of the road in front of the Dak Bungalow and started selling colourful trinkets like bangles and hair clips. A flutewallah appeared. And finally some enterprising soul wheeled in a creaky wooden merry go round that had small plastic cars for seats. Everybody seemed to be having fun.

Finally I saw Kammu chatting with a couple of policemen in the corner of the veranda. For a long time, I tried to catch Kammu's eyes through the crowd. After ages he turned from where he was gossiping with the policemen, and looked at me. I raised my eyebrows at Kammu and frowned. He waggled his eyebrows back at me. I went and stood at the other corner of the veranda, holding my 'clue'. Kammu came up.

'Since when have the cops become such great friend of yours?' I snapped, feeling irritable. 'I've been waiting for years to discuss our clue!'

Kammu looked guilty. 'These police not too bad.' He said apologetically. 'They gave me *gutka*.'

'*Gutka* will kill you,' I scolded him as I handed my clue to him. It looked like a piece of rubber, only it was skin coloured. And it was also thin, like a kind of membrane.

'What do you think this is?' I asked him.

'Rubber'

'Eat more *gutka*. It will stimulate your brain.' I was being as sarcastic as I could. 'Even I know it is rubber. But what is it?'

'You should have left it for police,' Kammu scolded in a hoarse whisper. 'They will know what it is. Now they arrest you.'

'How are they going to arrest me? Are you going to tell them,' I challenged him, suddenly feeling close to tears. I knew I shouldn't have picked up the clue, but at that time I just wasn't thinking. 'And they jolly well won't know what it is,' I insisted. 'If we don't know, they can't tell either.'

At that moment, Dad came up and put his arm around me. 'How are you Andu?' he said, his eyes anxious. 'I'm glad Kammu is looking after you.' He saw the piece of rubber I was holding in my hand. 'I'm thankful to see you're playing, to keep your mind off this horrible thing,' he said. 'I didn't know you had brought your Hanuman mask along with you. How did you tear it?'

Kammu and I stared at him, speechless, our eyes suddenly gleaming with excitement. And then we looked at each other. We both knew what the other was thinking. That the murderer had worn a mask! One of those cheap latex masks that was available in any cheap toy shop for ten rupees. And Haru had torn away a piece of it, in a struggle, probably, before he died.

'Z'

I sat in the chair on the veranda beside Mom for god knows how long. My mind must have switched off for quite some time because the next thing I remember was that Mom had fallen asleep in her chair, and that I was feeling very hungry.

It must have been a shock to Mom, that dead body in her room. And after having spent a night drugged by that horrid...I was feeling too hungry to think. I needed my chicken curry. It must be time for lunch, I thought, groggily.

The next moment, a small explosion happened in my head and I woke up and sat up straight in my chair. I mean, an idea exploded inside my head. An idea which cleared my mind of all sleep.

Last night Jamir had gone to meet the Deputy. And then he must have come back here. And today this murder...and this chaos...and such a lot of people had been tramping in and out of the bungalow since Dad had called the police...but I didn't remember seeing Jamir. He should have been the first one to be caught and questioned, I thought.

I looked across the overgrown garden towards Jamir's quarters. Where was Jamir? I looked sideways at Mom. She was snoring slightly. Dad was nowhere to be seen. The murmuring of quiet voices came from my room. Probably Dad and the authorities were discussing their stuff in my room. Kammu also wasn't to be seen. He was possibly asleep in the car. I got up and slowly descended the steps towards Jamir's quarters. I had not gone there before, but had seen his room through the overgrown bushes from when we were taking our bath at the well on our first morning here.

Jamir's house was built as an outhouse—a simple shack like brick structure with a red broken-tiled roof with steps leading up to the closed front door. As I neared the place, the grass seemed to crunch loudly underfoot, and I was aware of the deep silence of the midday. The sun was hot. The dull green peeling paint of the termite eaten door made me feel a little sick. Ugly mossy bricks showed through the cracked plaster of the walls. The steps were also cracked. A peepal tree had taken root in the crack of the third stair and had sent out delicate greenish pink leaves. Very young, whole leaves. I suddenly thought that this village was a lot like this little plant. On the surface it was like a dream, afresh wholesome Indian village, but underneath were the cracks...and the blind white slugs that lived under them, protected in the dark. What kind of slug was I about to uncover?

The door wasn't locked. I pushed it open. It was dim and musty inside and smelt faintly of beedi smoke. I looked around. The first thing that struck me was that the room was very neat and clean. Not a speck of dust showed on the floor. Not a cobweb hung on the ceiling. There was a charpoy with a neatly folded chaddar on a sad looking pillow at the head. It would be the head of the bed, if it was against the wall opposite the door, right? The foot of the bed would be towards the door, towards me. On the left hand side of the cot, I mean if you were lying on the cot, that is, was a small plastic stool on which was an earthen pot covered with a small flat earthen plate. Water, I guessed. There was an upturned aluminum glass on the jar.

On the right was a small grey steel cupboard. I tried to open it. Maybe I shouldn't have, but if you were in my place, you would have, I bet. It was locked. I looked around the room. Jamir didn't seem the kind of man who would carry a key around with him. I looked at the upturned aluminum glass. If I was Jamir...I walked towards the pot and lifted the glass off its top. Aha! The key was right there.

I cannot imagine how a man can be so neat. I stood staring at the contents of the cupboard, feeling strangely uneasy. There were a few clothes, a couple of lungis and kurtas, a thick brown sweater, a monkey cap and a few other assorted mufflers and blankets. Everything was very old and shabby, the colours almost leached out to a sort of uniform greyish-blue. As I lifted the items gingerly one by one, I saw that a few were torn but carefully stitched up with tiny even stitches, and each thing was folded neatly and kept away layer on layer, completely and utterly tidily. Not even Dadudida's cupboards are so neat, and that's saying something. I suddenly felt guilty.But I still decided to open the closed drawer anyway. I pulled it gently open and got a shock. Stacked neatly in the drawer was a dozen or so of handkerchiefs. And the topmost one had the letter 'Z' embroidered on it.

I delicately poked about and lifted each handkerchief. Each of them had the same letter Z sewn on in different colours. And underneath the pile of hankies was something square and hard. My hand was shaking as I pulled it out slowly. It was a photograph. It was a very old framed photograph, yellow and slightly stained. It showed a very young Jamir, about 14 or 15 years old—I guessed it was Jamir, the features were the same—and a young girl in a wheelchair, holding hands and staring at the camera. The girl was about 7 or 8 years old. She was smiling sweetly but Jamir looked very serious. She looked a bit like Jamir, too. I could also faintly make out the blurry shape of a sewing machine in the corner. The sewing machine looked familiar. I peered at it.

It looked like the ancient Singer sewing machine which Dadudida had.

I was staring at the photograph and then suddenly, with a shock I realised that this must be Jamir's sister and she must have embroidered these handkerchiefs for him. But Z? And then another jolt of electricity seemed to pass through me. NOT Jamir, my brain screamed. *Zameer* was the guy's name! In English, it would be spelt with Z!

And then the world became black.

Sacked!

I don't mean that someone bonked me on the head and I switched off like the detective in the general mystery stories that one gets to read. And also like these mystery stories, I didn't suddenly recover consciousness with a groan, rub my rapidly swelling head gingerly, flutter my eyes and say, 'Where am I?'

What really happened was this:

Here I was, happily standing in front of Jamir's cupboard and snooping away to glory, while behind me, the door lay wide open for anyone to peek in and see me engaged upon my utterly illegal activities. Someone obviously saw, and that someone creeped up behind me as I was peering at Jamir's old family photo, and that someone covered my head in one sweep from behind me with a kind of scratchy black cloth, pinning my hands to my sides and tying it around my middle in one deft movement just as I exclaimed, Zameer!

Looking back, I can say that it served me right. I should be more careful when engaged in illegal activities, and the least I could have done was to shut the door behind me. But at that time, I let out a mighty yell and started hopping, trying to release my arms. It was terribly scratchy—the cloth. And it smelt of garlic. Ooh. The memory still makes me shudder. My face and upper arms itched all over.

'Shut up,' snarled a hoarse voice in my ear.

'Jamirbhai?' I called, a little uncertainly.

'Shut up or I'll bash your brains out.' The smell of garlic was driving me crazy.

I stopped jumping and stood quite still. I remember, I almost stopped breathing. What if the guy was serious? You never know with these people. I remembered the first night at the Dak Bungalow and the way his eyes had glittered his hate at us. I didn't want to die with my brains oozing out inside a scratchy garlicky sack.

'Interfering pests! A whole family of interfering pests. I won't let you spoil my plans, you hear? I'll kill you before that. Just shut up and do what I say.'

'Okay,' I quavered. Nothing brilliant occurred to me.

'Just shut up and wait here. Understand?' growled Jamir in my ear.

'I said okay already!' I was beginning to feel hysterical. How many times was I supposed to agree with this madman?

Jamir silently hustled me out of the house and onto a bicycle, muttering threats into my ears all the while.

I tried to cling on to the back of the bike as best as I could while Jamir went bumping along. I was suffocating inside the sack and the bumps and jolts were making me feel pukey. I lost all sense of direction. Sometimes I felt that the bicycle was a hundred feet high and that I was sitting way above the ground and the thought of being at such a height began to make me feel dizzy. I held on to my puke as best as I could, and I clung on to the bike as best as I could. After I don't know how long, Jamir stopped. 'Here we are,' he said. 'Get off.'

I got off, my legs feeling like jelly and my chest feeling like it was bursting for lack of air, and there was a sort of roaring inside my ears and all the sounds suddenly began to fade and *this* time, I guess, I really did faint.

In Saheb Bagan again

I woke up, feeling something cool pressing against my cheeks. My face and arms felt like they were on fire.

'OOOh!' I said, opening my eyes. 'Everything itches.'

Jamir's face loomed over mine, darkly menacing. He was blocking my view, so I couldn't make out where I was. I shrank back, feeling a little scared. I was feeling too weak to pretend to be brave in front of him, and I didn't want to burst into tears so he could crow over me or bully me any more than he already was.

But strangely enough, Jamir pressed the cool, wet cloth to my cheeks, very gently. I blinked up at him, and lifted my hand, trying to scratch my face. He took my hand and laid it down on my chest.

'Don't,' he said, 'you'll only make it worse.'

I stared at him. 'Why are you being so nice to me all of a sudden?' I asked suspiciously, struggling to sit up. I looked around the dim room. It was a room of what looked like an old bungalow, with large French windows, obviously closed, and a high wooden ceiling. An old bulbous looking fan was on, making a steady rattling noise and wobbling dangerously as it rotated. And I was lying on the floor on a mattress, with a pillow and sheets and everything. All along the walls were more mattresses, and in a corner, was a pile of blankets and pillows. It looked like a dormitory.

'I am in the bungalow of Saheb Bagan, aren't I?' I asked Jamir, aware that he was watching me keenly. He nodded. 'Why did you kidnap me?'

Jamir winced. 'I don't like the word kidnap,' he said, and his voice suddenly sounded younger, stronger. He looked different, too. Not so...old.

'You're not as old as you act,' I blurted out.

'Right. I'm forty-five. Not sixty. It is easy to fool villagers. White hair, limp, hoarse voice, pan masala, spitting...and anyway, nobody came to the Dak Bungalow and I rarely went into the village. So it was easy to pretend,' he said in an expressionless voice.

'That girl in the photograph...'

'My sister. I worked hard after my parents died. No one helped us. I earned money, sent her to an English school.' His eyes glowed when he spoke of her. I guessed that he loved her very much.

'So she's the one who embroidered the handkerchiefs?'

He nodded.

'But what will she think if she knew you are a kidnapper?' I asked, irritably, screwing up my face because of the terrible itch.

'Here, take this,' said Jamir, handing me the wet handkerchief. I put it to my face. The itch began to subside.

'I am worse than a kidnapper,' said Jamir, when he saw that I was feeling a bit comfortable. 'And I don't care.' He said it softly, sadly.

Something inside my heart quivered. I said, 'but your sister ...'

'She is in no position to know. They have her hostage. I have to do as they say. I don't even get to talk to her. Every week they bring me a new handkerchief, so I know she is alive.'

'Who are "they"?' I whispered. 'What do they make you do?' I asked, my mind flashing back to the Deputy DM's study, where Jamir had gone to meet him last night.

'They are terrible people. Smugglers. I do whatever they tell me.'

'What do they smuggle?'

'Come with me,' said Jamir, getting up. I got up and followed him out of the room and down a hall with closed doors on either side. When we reached the end of the hall, he flung open the door and gestured for me to go inside.

I went inside and stopped. On the floor of the room, on rows of mattresses, there lay about ten children of about my age or younger, sprawled about. All of them seemed to be deeply asleep.

'Children,' he said.

Smuggled Goods

I stared at the sleeping kids uncomprehendingly. My brain seemed to have jammed.

'Children?' I looked at Jamirbhai and shook my head. 'I don't understand.'

Jamirbhai shut the door and turned. 'Come to the other room, I'll explain.'

In the other room, Jamirbhai made himself comfortable by leaning against the pile of pillows. I sat next to him.

'These children,' he began, 'are from Bangladesh. They come from very poor families. Their parents are told that they will be able to get good jobs in India. Most parents agree to send their children with these "agents", as they call themselves. They are then smuggled into India by *them* and kept here, in this house. Then they are sent to various factories or houses to work. Every month, one man from the gang goes to each of these houses to collect the money that the child earns. The money goes into their pockets. It is a huge racket.'

'My God.' I still couldn't believe it. 'How long has this been going on?'

'Two years,' Jamirbhai sighed.

'And you have been helping them all this while?' I was so angry, I forgot my itchy face.

'What to do.' He turned his hands, palm upwards. 'I was forced.'

'What *do* you do, exactly?' I asked.

'I cook their meals and generally look after them while they are here. I am supposed to keep them locked up and see that they don't run away while suitable jobs are being found for them.'

Something flashed in my mind. 'Oh!' I cried, 'The chickens! *That's* why you cook so many chickens every day.'

Jamirbhai nodded. 'Yes. It keeps them happy as they don't have the money for much more than a dal or a vegetable with rice at home. It makes them keep quiet and they feel that they will have a good life in India.'

'How could you?' I cried, I was almost crying and I didn't care if Jamirbhai saw it.

'What would you have done if they kidnapped your sister?' he said harshly.

'I am also a Bangladeshi. Sometimes I used to slip into India to steal a few things from the railway goods wagons at the railway siding to make a bit of money. One day, I got caught. I was told that if I listened to them, I would not go to jail. At first I too thought that the children were going to have a happier life. But when I realised that they were stealing all the children's money, I rebelled. I threatened to go to the police. Then they kidnapped my sister.'

'You were stupid.' I was very angry now and didn't care that Jamirbhai was way older. 'You should have gone to the police instead of letting them know what you were going to do,' I said.

'Don't you think I know that,' said Jamirbhai bitterly. 'How many times have I regretted losing my head that day, I've lost count. But they have so many policemen in their pockets whom to go to, I don't know.'

'So why did you kidnap me? What will it achieve?'

'I'm scared,' said Jamirbhai, looking down. His hands were shaking. 'I saw you in my room and thought if I let you go, you would call the police. After Haru's murder, I don't know what to think. He told me he would protect us.'

'Who told you he would protect you?'

'The Deputy DM. He's been trying to catch the mastermind red handed. Haru Tantrik worked as go between. The gang trusted him, but he was a good man. He would pass on messages to the DM. He looked like a tantrik, could go anywhere, find out what was happening.' Jamirbhai's voice rose.

'He is the one who told me that the Deputy would help me if I helped him to catch the kingpin.' Jamirbhai wrung his hands. His voice rose another notch. 'But now, they have murdered Haru. How will the Deputy protect me? He couldn't protect Haru!' Jamirbhai had begun to sound hysterical.

'Wait wait wait,' my head was buzzing. 'You mean the Deputy DM is the *good* guy? And that he knows that there are children being smuggled?' Jamirbhai nodded.

'You mean he knows that there are children here, now?'

Jamirbhai again nodded. He looked acutely unhappy.

'And he is doing nothing?'

'No. He is doing something. We were about to lay a trap for the leader of the gang to come here. Then we would have caught him red handed. Otherwise, he will go elsewhere and start this sort of thing again!'

'And what was the trap?'

'I don't know,' Jamirbhai wailed.

'The Deputy was getting a group of trusted men together. And then you people came to shoot ghosts, and everything became *ulta-pulta*.' He glared accusingly at me.

'Haru got murdered, and now I don't know what to do. The police will catch me, and the Deputy DM can't do anything—he can't catch the ringleader, and he can't save me.' Jamirbhai's voice broke.

'The Deputy tried to stop you people from coming to Saheb Bagan at night by locking you up in his house. He was afraid you might spoil his plans.'

'But why do you think Haru Tantrik came to the Dak Bungalow at night?'

'Maybe to warn you not to go to Saheb Bagan. He couldn't have known that the Deputy DM would be successful in keeping all of you locked up in his house for the night. We wanted to protect all of you. It was our problem, why should an innocent family suffer? If you people had come here, do you think they would have let you leave this place alive?'

I felt tears prick my eyes. So many people had tried to look out for us. And one man had been killed for that.

'But if you don't know the kingpin, who do you take orders from?' I asked. I suddenly wanted to know everything. If I knew everything, I felt that I might find a way, any way to get us all out of this mess.

Jamirbhai got up and began to pace up and down.

'See, Bablu's father is the one who smuggles the children out of Bangladesh with the help of his Bangladeshi friends. The man in the marketplace who owns the rice plate shop used to pass on the messages to Haru, and Haru came and told me how many children were coming and when they had to be kept ready for transport to the city.'

'Bablu's father! The Riceplate Man! No wonder Bablu's father was sleeping that day—he had made a night trip to get new children!' I remembered that day in the marketplace.

'Bablu hadn't known that he had come back! And Haru and you worked as double agents? Is *everybody* in this village involved in this horrible thing?' My head reeled.

Jamirbhai smiled wanly. 'It does seem like that, doesn't it?'

'So now that Haru has been murdered, don't you think the gang will want to spirit the children away tonight? Why should they take a risk and keep the children here?'

I was trying hard to think. 'I mean, if I was the gang's kingpin, and somebody got murdered near a place where I was doing something fishy, I would surely want to shift my base of operations from there, wouldn't I? The police might stumble upon it any minute!'

Jamirbhai slowly nodded. 'You're right. The gang will come for the children tonight. I should have thought of that. What should we do?' and Jamirbhai looked at me hopefully.

My mind became blank. 'I'm hungry,' I told Jamirbhai. 'I can't think.'

Chicken and Plans

I took off my shirt and helped Jamirbhai to cook lunch.

For one fleeting moment I thought of going to my folks with this story. Then I pushed the thought away from my head.

I knew what would happen if I went to them. They would forbid me to get involved, and would go to the police. Jamirbhai had said that many of the cops, too, were involved in this racket. Just to show that they had done something, maybe they would rescue the children this one time, but what would happen to Jamirbhai's sister? And the kingpin would surely escape, and set up another smuggling racket in another part of the border. No, I couldn't tell Mom and Dad anything about this, yet. Not if we were to catch the kingpin red handed.

Jamirbhai told me that he fed the kids once a day. Then they were made to have their sleeping potion and sleep for the rest of the day again. I was appalled. As I was helping Jamirbhai to cook the chicken over a wood fire, I gave him a few reproachful glances. I wanted to go into all the 'How *could* you's' and the 'Didn't you once *feel*' kind of stuff again, but Jamirbhai was looking so woebegone that I actually ended up feeling more sorry for him than ever.

After the rice and chicken were cooked, we woke the kids and all of us sat down to eat together. By that time my head was buzzing with hunger, and the smoky wooden taste mingled with the curry tasted completely out of this world. As I was eating, I suddenly felt that I must be a very insensitive person. Here were we, sitting with a bunch of half starved, drugged children who had been all but kidnapped from their homes by a ruthless murderer, their futures completely uncertain, and Jamirbhai's poor crippled sister a hostage, and I was sitting here enjoying the woodsmoke smell in my chicken curry! I must be a complete and utter brute.

This thought so demoralised me, that after lunch, when we had all washed up and everybody was feeling pleasantly full, I couldn't think of a single idea.

When Jamirbhai looked at me hopefully and asked, 'Now, tell us what to do,' I just felt terribly dull and blank. For want of anything better, I stuttered, 'Can't we all go to the police?' Jamirbhai looked at me sadly. 'Then I'll never see my sister again.'

After that I went for a walk around the house with Jamirbhai, 'to clear my mind' I told him, while the other kids huddled together, desultorily chatting amongst themselves, still too drowsy to do anything more active.

That was when I saw the bear cub.

I stopped and stared. It was chained to the post of an unused tubewell at the back of the bungalow.

'This was what chased Kammu and me that night,' I breathed. 'The green monster!'

'That was glow-paint,' explained Jamirbhai sheepishly. 'Bablu's father brought it for me. He said it would glow in the dark, and that would scare any stray beggar or villager who came in here by mistake if we smeared it on our faces and pretended to beghosts. The bear got loose and found the stash of paint. He upset a can over his face... ' Jamirbhai shrugged.

'But how did you get the bear?' I asked.

'I found the bear a few months ago in the jungle there,' Jamirbhai said waving his arm. 'It was injured. I looked after it, and since then it's become quite tame. I keep him chained up here, since I don't want him to slip into the house while the children are asleep. You never know, they might get scared and hurt it.'

'Is it tame?' I asked doubtfully.

'It is,' said Jamirbhai, smiling faintly, 'anyway, it's never hurt me.' He lifted his hand to stroke the bear's shaggy head, and the bear gave a sort of quiver of ecstasy and rolled over like a great shaggy ball.

I laughed, it looked so comical. How could I have thought it to be savage? 'It's still very young, isn't it?' I asked, 'It still wants to play. So why do you keep it chained like that?'

'Suppose someone scares him?' said Jamirbhai, tickling the bear on its tummy. 'It might hurt them then. How scared you were that night,' laughed Jamirbhai. 'He just wanted to play. I was afraid you people would hurt him.'

I remembered that night and felt a bit sheepish. 'How did you manage the green fog and the mist?' I asked hastily, changing the topic.

'Those were fog and mist machines...just to...you know...make it look ghostly. Bablu's father installed them.'

I began to feel utterly stupid. I had been conned by a tame bear cub and a stupid fog machine and I now felt ashamed to think how Kammu and I had run for our lives that day.

And it was then that the plan finally occurred to me...

The Kingpin comes

I tore my vest and dirtied my face with a little mud. I had also slicked back my hair with the coconut oil that Jamirbhai had given me so that my crew cut wouldn't show so much. I hoped I would pass off as one of the Bangladeshi boys. And while I waited behind the bushes and swatted at the mosquitoes,

I tried to remember how Dadudida sounded when they were excited and spoke in their Bangladeshi dialect...

As it slowly grew dark and the shadows closed in, I began to worry. I had instructed the other boys to each choose a bush and hide behind it. Would they stay hidden, or would they try to get back to Saheb Bagan? There hadn't been time to explain everything to them. And even if there had been, I doubted whether they would understand. As it is, they found it difficult to follow my accent, and I found it difficult to follow their different dialects.

Also, would Jamirbhai be able to act convincingly enough? Everything hinged on his being able to convince Bablu's father and the Riceplate Man that all the children had escaped.

The fireflies began coming out in ones and twos, and the buzzing of the mosquitoes in my ear grew louder and more persistent so that it seemed that the noise was inside my head. I scratched and swatted and almost missed the faint hubbub that was growing louder and louder and coming nearer. Finally it was unmistakable. The crashing sound of men running through bushes, the muffled instructions that they shouted to each other, the faint bobbing light of the torches they carried—they had finally come to find us!

I heard squeals and curses as the boys were discovered hiding in the jungle, and I could, through my cover behind my bush, see a few of them actually putting up a convincing struggle when they were caught. I was so intent on watching them, that I was taken completely aback when someone shone a torch into my face.

'Here's one more!' shouted a voice and I felt my arm being taken in a firm grip. I struggled, and the man tightened his grip. It hurt and I moaned. 'Shuddup,' hissed the voice in my ear. The man then dragged me out from the bushes towards a clearing near Saheb Bagan where the other boys were standing huddled together. I stumbled and followed him, the man pulling my arm so hard that it's a wonder it wasn't wrenched out from its socket by the time he flung me into the crowd. Some of the boys were sobbing in bewilderment and fright. I felt sorry for them—they could hardly understand what was going on—but I didn't dare speak to them, out of fear they might give away the fact that I wasn't one of them.

I saw Jamirbhai and a couple of other hard faced men guarding us, while Bablu's father and the Riceplate Man continued looking for the other boys who had still not been found. Jamirbhai didn't look at me, and I didn't look at him. One of the men looked at his watch and growled something to his companion.

But nothing happened. We still stood there in the dark in the clearing, huddled together and miserable, the mosquitoes singing their monotonous bloodthirsty chorus in our ears.

After ages, I heard the faint sound of an engine, soon followed by a pair of headlights shining through the undergrowth of the jungle. The truck was covered on the top and sides with tarpaulin. As everyone watched the truck drive up...

'He's come,' hissed a voice in my ear.

'Jamirbhai!' I looked up at him, 'don't talk to me, what if they see you?'

'They're watching the truck. But are you sure you want to go along? Because, I haven't been able to tell the Deputy... '

My heart sank. 'Tell him after we leave,' I hissed.

'But we won't know where these people will take you,' Jamirbhai hissed back, urgently.

'Jamir, you fool,' snarled one of the men. 'Start loading the kids. What are you standing there for? It was all because you were stupid enough to let the kids run away that we've had to go through this useless rigmarole.'

Jamirda started whining something in a plaintive voice about how it wasn't his fault while shooing us towards the truck and my spirits lifted a little. Boy, could he act!

Now I had to do my part.

As the men pushed us towards the open back of the truck, I stumbled and fell with a loud yell. A couple of the men rushed towards me while I lay on the ground and writhed in agony. I held my leg and I sobbed and screamed and cried and raised merry hell. 'I think I've been bitten by a snake!' I bawled at the top of my voice, trying to sound like a Bangladeshi, screwing up my face horribly so that the Riceplate Man wouldn't recognise me.

'Shut up!' snarled one of the men giving me a cuff on my head. My head rang and I saw green stars. I opened my mouth to shout louder, while another man quickly clamped his hand over my mouth. I promptly bit him as hard as I could. The man gave a yell, and quickly jumped away from me.

'What is happening here?' It was the iciest, scariest voice I have ever heard in my life. It cut across all our noise and drama like a sharp knife. I swallowed my yell. The man whom I had bitten nursed his hand, glaring at me balefully, but he, too, did not speak.

I looked up, my face still screwed up horribly in a grimace, and my heart lurched in my chest.

For I was looking into a hairy, wrinkled, grotesque face, indirectly illuminated by the couple of torches that the gang members held in their hands.

With mounting panic, I realised that this terribly

disfigured face could not possibly be human.

Then the face spoke again. It thrust its head out at me and said, 'If you shout again, I'll kill you.' I saw that his lips weren't moving and suddenly realised that the face belonged to a human and that the man was wearing a mask. It was the half light that had made my mind freak. Goosebumps came out all over my body and I shivered. Here he was, finally—my masked man!

As they dragged me roughly towards the truck, I tried to look back at Jamirbhai to see whether he'd been able to do what I had told him. I thought I saw him giving me a faint nod before the men thrust me into the truck. I fell hard on the floor and moaned in pain. My elbow hurt. By the time I struggled to sit up, the truck's tailboard was raised, a roll of tarpaulin dropped down from the top to cover the back, and it was jolting along the rough dirt road into pitch darkness. We were off!

In the darkness

I sat up on the floor of the truck and sniffed. I could smell the faint bear smell. As my eyes got adjusted to the dark, I saw that the children were huddled in one corner. They were all staring fearfully at a ball of concentrated darkness in the far opposite corner. I heard a faint whimper. The bear was scared. I crawled over the lurching floor of the truck towards it and sat down beside it with my arms around its neck. It huddled close to me and its rough hairs scratched my bare legs.

'You're not afraid?' asked one of the children. I could just about understand his dialect.

'No,' I said and then explained to them what I was about to do, and what I expected them to do.

The tarpaulin had been pulled down, and I couldn't see where we were, but I could feel that the truck had put on speed. I started counting seconds. When I had counted about twenty minutes approximately, I slowly stood up and balanced myself by holding on to the side of the truck. The bear clung on to my leg and I could feel its sharp claws gently digging into me.

I inched towards the little glass window behind the driver's cabin, holding on to the sides of the truck, dragging the bear along with me. Just before I reached it, I crouched down and pulled the bear up. It stood up on its hind legs, still clinging on to my right leg with its forepaws. I dug into my pocket and pulled out the little tin can. I dipped my fingers in it and rubbed a little on the bear's face gently so that it did not get into its eyes. The bear stood still while I was doing this and afterwards it lightly butted me on my chest with its head. It thought it was a game. I took hold of his paws and rubbed the paint on them too. Then I placed his paws on the cabin window and ducked back behind its hairy body. And then I began to hammer on the wall separating us from the driver's cabin with all my might. The other children lined up beside me and began hammering on the partition wall, too.

The bear thought it was a game and joined in. It, too, hammered on the glass partition, its mouth open and saliva dripping down. The paint glowed eerily on its face and paws in the faint light of the glowing dials of the driver's cabin. It would give them a shock when they looked back. I was counting on it.

After a while, I thought I heard faint shouts and felt the truck slowing down and finally stopping. The back of the truck was thrown open and a torch shone inside.

'Now!' I shouted, and all of us together, including the bear, rushed out of the truck and jumped down to the ground. Unfortunately for the man with the torch, the bear landed partly on him, and I heard a sudden, muffled yell. I looked around and saw that the man with the torch was the masked man. The bear was drooling all over his face, while he was trying to ward him off. The torch had fallen out of his hands and was rolling to and fro in the grass, and in its light, I saw the faint glint of his ring as the masked man lifted his hands to protect his face. The other man who was with him was running hard towards the thick jungle that lined the road, the boys after him, yelling lustily.

I ran to the front of the truck and wrenched open the door on the driver's side. As long as everyone was scattered all over the countryside, it was okay. I just had to prevent the masked man from driving away with the truck. He *had* to stay here. I had to make sure of that. But the masked man had seen me! He heaved the bear off himself and came running after me, cursing loudly.

I jumped into the driver's seat and tried to turn the key which still hung in the ignition. My hand was shaking so much that it slipped and fell. As I bent down to retrieve it, he threw open the door to the driver's cabin and grabbed at me, trying to pull me out of the truck. I shouted and struggled, clinging on to the steering wheel with all my strength, but he was far stronger that I was. The man lunged at me again. He grabbed my shoulder hard, almost dislocating it. I twisted around and bit him. He let go of me with a yell. I saw the key on the floor and bent down to pick it up. The man lunged at me again. I felt a ringing blow on my head and stars danced in front of my eyes.

I clutched the key hard in my hand. It bit into my palm and the pain cleared my head. I tried pushing the key into the ignition again. This time it went in and I looked around, expecting another blow. But what I saw outside was a strange sight.

The bear, furious at being flung away like that in the middle of what it had thought was a friendly game, had attacked the masked man from behind. The man was now trying to fight him off, leaving me free to start the truck. As man and bear fought, I turned the ignition and started the truck. Kammu had given me illegal driving lessons early in the mornings on the way to school, but this was a far cry from driving a car. I pressed the clutch, changed the gear and pressed the accelerator and the truck lurched forward. I heard a yell and looked back to see the masked man running after the truck, and the bear lumbering after him. The truck coughed and stalled and I tried to start it again. The masked man was catching up! As the truck started again, I saw, in my rear view mirror, flashing lights of a police car. After a while, the comforting sound of sirens filled the night. I stopped the truck with a sigh of relief. But the masked man was nowhere in sight!

He had melted away into the night.

The Last Clue

There were three police jeeps. Mom and Dad were with the Deputy DM and Mr. Das in one of them. They made a great deal of fuss over me as the constables rounded off the boys and the companion of the masked man. I heard that as soon as we were off, Jamirbhai had given the other gang members the slip and had biked over to the Deputy.

Mom told me that the Riceplate Man and Bablu's father were in police custody. They had told the police which route we were likely to take. But I still felt bad that I had let the kingpin escape.

'The bear has been found!' said Mr. Deputy excitedly as he toddled up to us.

'The bear? He hasn't been hurt, has he?' I was anxious.

'No sir. Hale and hearty. He is with Harish constable.' The Deputy DM was beaming excitedly and his words tumbled over each other as he spoke to me. 'Your plan was igeeniuss, extremely ingeeniuss, master Anand! It was not your fault the leader escaped.'

I looked up at his honest, perspiring face and thought how foolish I had been to suspect him. He had genuinely wanted to catch the kingpin red handed and I had messed it up. And he was being so gracious about it all. Why suspect a man just because he was fond of the colour pink?

Mr. Das now came forward and whispered solemnly to his right foot. 'Mr. Anand. We are very grateful.' He took out a card and gave it to me. It read; Mr. H. R. Das, Deputy Attache, Bangladesh Government. 'Oh!' I said, looking up at him. He nodded gravely at the bush to my right. 'We have been trying to catch this gang for a long time now. And you have helped us do it. My country is very grateful.' And he gave a small jerky bow. As he was turning away, I clutched his arm. 'Mr. Das?' This time he almost looked at me. 'We haven't yet caught the kingpin. What if he hurts Jamir's sister? Can you make sure she is all right?' He nodded. 'We shall do our best. And when we find her, all will be forgiven and forgotten,' he said to my right ear. And I had to be content with that.

But Mom wasn't so forgiving, 'You could have been hurt, Andu. Next time don't try these stunts. Just tell us.'

Suddenly an excited babble of voices broke out. A group of policemen were escorting someone over to the police jeep where we were standing.

'Jiten!' Dad was astonished. 'How come you're here!'

Jitenkaku was in a sorry state. He was limping. His shirt was torn. 'The masked man got away!' he gasped.

The Deputy DM looked surprised. 'But we thought you were in Kolkata!'

'I was. But I came to see my friends here, after I heard about Haru Tantrik's murder. I thought they might be in trouble. And I was right!'

'We're not in trouble!' I was indignant. 'Anyway, how did you know we were *here*?'

'I have my people,' Jitenkaku was being exasperatingly mysterious. He looked at the Deputy accusingly, 'You should have informed me about all this!'

Before the Deputy could respond, we heard a shout and someone pushed his head inside our circle. Mom gave a yell. It was a black, shaggy head, still glowing faintly green. Harish constable had been a little lax with his charge and the bear had lumbered up to our group to see what was up.

The bear came up to me and butted me gently on the chest. I laughed and put my arms around it.

'It might have nits!' Mom cried. 'Andu let it go!'

The bear looked around our group. At Mom and Dad and Harish constable standing a little outside, and the Deputy. He gave a small grunt as his eyes alighted on Jitenkaku, and the bear pushed me gently away and began walking towards him, making a low, growling noise in its throat. Jitenkaku's eyes widened and he held out his hands as if to ward off the bear. It was then that my eyes caught the glint of metal again.

'Mom! Dad!' I shouted, 'Jitenkaku's the kingpin. He's the masked man.'

Everybody froze. The bear continued to advance. Jitenkaku started backing away slowly. 'What nonsense!' he said, 'this boy is mad. And so is the bear. I am the District Magistrate of this area. Call the bear off.' The last sentence was like a whiplash.

I saw Harish constable hesitate.

'The bear is angry with him because he fought with it! Look at the scratches on his hands!' I shouted. I *had* to convince them. 'Look at his ring! The masked man was wearing this ring! The snake with ruby eyes eating its own tail. I saw it! I tell you I saw it! And you'll probably find the mask in his pocket! He murdered Haru Tantrik.'

With a roar Harish constable fell upon Jiten kaku. The other policemen came running up. In the scuffle, the mask fell out of Jitenkaku's pocket.

And at the same instant, Kammu drew up in our car.

'The mask!' he cried, running up to us, 'you found the mask of murderer!'

'What mask of murderer?' Mom was completely at sea.

'You no tell them Haru's killer wore mask?'

Kammu asked me.

'When did I have the chance!' I shouted at Kammu, suddenly feeling very very tired. 'I just found out that Jitenkaku is the kingpin!'

I pulled the piece of rubber I had picked up from Haru Tantrik's dead body. 'See, this torn piece matches the torn area of the mask just behind the ear. Look! I found it on Haru Tantrik's body.'

The Deputy DM squatted in front of me. 'But you shouldn't have taken it from the body, Master Anand,' he said, shaking his head reprovingly.

'He not take. I take,' lied Kammu. He knew Mom and Dad would give me hell over this. 'I am not knowing these things. I gave him to keep. He don't tell police to save me.'

'But I don't understand one thing,' Dad was still looking puzzled. 'Why did Jiten pretend that he fought with the masked man just now?'

'It's simple,' I said, leaning my head against the police jeep. 'He was trying to run away. One of the policemen must have seen him while rounding up the kids. So to explain away his presence here, he had to pretend that he had been here somehow from the beginning and that he had fought with the masked man. Just to divert suspicion away from himself.'

'I see him Saab!' Harish constable saluted the Deputy. 'He running in forest. I say "Halt!" Then I see it is Magistrate Saab. He say masked man escape, and he running to catch him. But I am glad culprit caught. Haru Tantrik good man. My friend. Why he kill good man, I don't know.'

'Yes, why?' asked Kammu turning towards me.

'What am I, a witch doctor?' I snapped. I just wanted to sleep. 'Haru must have found out the masked man's identity. The mask was torn, remember? Haru must have wrenched it off Jitenkaku's face. So Jitenkaku had to kill him.'

Dad and Mom bundled me into our car. I was almost nodding off when a picture flashed into my mind. A picture of an old man under a tree. 'Oh, by the way,' I muttered, just about dragging my eyelids open, 'that old man under the tree was also Jitenkaku in disguise. When he wanted to keep an eye on things, he used to dress up like that.'

Dad and Mom didn't say anything. As we were driving away, I heard Dad mutter, 'I wish Jiten hadn't told us about Saheb Bagan and the ghosts. I don't want us to get involved in this sort of thing.'

'Jitenkaku told us because...' I could hardly form the words, '...he was proud. No one knew of his cleverness. Pride. All criminals have...' And I fell fast asleep.